Amphitrite

The Forbidden, Volume 1

Shaine Lake

Published by Shaine Lake, 2016.

Amphitrite

Shaine Lake

Published by Shaine Lake

Discover *The Forbidden* Trilogy:

Book of Metamorphosis - Amphitrite

Book of Redemption - Beast within the Man

Book of Damnation - Cimmerian

Book Cover Design, Effects and Layout by Shaine Lake

Photographs (CC BY 2.0) by tata_aka_T, Tanaka Juuyoh and Son of Groucho

Typeface by Dieter Steffmann

Wave Design and Printer's Ornaments by Lauren

Logo by Denise Clendenin

Chapter 1 Ripples

The sea looks breath-taking, yet dangers lurk within.
To preserve its beauty, the demon must be fed.

In the impenetrable darkness illuminated only by the fires blazing on top of few wooden sticks, the singing of the children punctured the unsettling silence to send off the procession.

Many gathered at the mouth of the village, and none uttered a word. Whether they were there to say their silent thanks and goodbyes to the sacrifice or just for the fun of it, only they themselves knew. A group of eight elders of the village, dressed in black cloaks, filed out of the opened ramshackle wooden gates, with each carrying a crude copper alloy lantern.

The sole figure in white robes was marching in front of the cortège. Concentrating on every step taken, she avoided eye contact with all, for a glance was all that she needed to regret her decision and flee away. As she traipsed towards the coast, the shrill voices of the children were gradually swallowed up by the dense, heavy, humid air, and the mud beneath her bare feet gave way to sand. When she was near the shoreline, the sounds of the waves cascading over each other assaulted her ears and reminded her of the utter cruelty of the demon, as told in the stories. But unnerved woman pressed on, holding onto the very belief that the foregoing of her life would save hundreds of villagers from the impending rampage.

After the procession hiked down a gentle rocky slope to reach the bottom, where the rocks were coated with algae and would be submerged in water during high tide, they beheld the sight of a colossal rock standing before them. Nailed to the top of the rock were a pair of long metal links, whose ends were adorned with rusted cuffs.

Under the dim, flicking light of the lanterns, the only young lady of the congregation lay her eyes on the countless splotches of dried blood smeared across the surface of that particular boulder. It was the corroboration for the gristly fate of the sacrifices before her. As her teeth chattered with trepidation, she was going to bolt out of the place when one of the elders—a middle-aged kind-looking man—grabbed her by the shoulders.

His usual amicable and friendly demeanour transmuted into one saturated with malice as he hissed, "You can't back out now. Our lives depend on you!"

"I want to live," cried the sacrifice. It was then she was shocked by her ability to speak.

A matronly woman shrieked, "Selfish girl! All of us will be eaten alive by *Ioteidas* if you run away!"

The other elders then rushed in to subdue the struggling lady and forcefully ram her wrists into the cuffs, yielding bruises in the process, before locking them.

"The sacrifice is now ready for your feasting," an elder yelled out to the spawning sea before him.

Then another one pulled out a dagger and carved a line from the sacrifice's wrist down to the inside of her elbow. The pain was unbearable.

Jolted out from the nightmare, Elsie stared at the ceiling wide-eyed. Notwithstanding the air-conditioning in her room, beads of sweat formed on her forehead. The stinging pain that ran down her forearm caused her to tremble in fright.

I thought it was just a dream?

Holding up her arm to observe the site of pain, she found no wound that could explain the pain. Sighing, she just had to assume it was all in the mind only. She did not expect the folk story told by the villagers would twine around her mind to worm its way into her dream.

The brave young man saving his maiden from being eaten by killing the demon that dwells in the darkest recesses of the sea. Just another fairy tale with happy ending. Why does it stay in my head?

Frustrated by the lack of plausible answers to her questions, twenty-four-year-old wiped the strands of her sweat-soaked dark auburn hair off her cheeks and got up from her bed to make her way to the bathroom.

I'd seen it all, been through it all. What's a nightmare to me?

En route to there, she snatched the remote control from the study table to switch on the television. Eager to get her dose of therapy through the splashes of water washing away her anxiety and the aftermath of the nightmare, she went on to step under the shower and let the cold sprinkles of water rained on her. Somehow, water had a soothing effect on her. She always had a love for lakes, rivers and oceans, which seemed to possess the magical power to take away the worries, along with the flow of the water. So naturally, her choice of location to go for vacation was Bantora village, an idyllic place by the sea, wedged between the bustling sea port at the South overseeing the Celtic Sea, and the west of Accastle, which was exposed to the exceptionally turbulent waters of the Atlantic Ocean.

"Accastle government is openly criticizing Mercales' total disregard of United Nations Convention on the Law of the Sea when Mercales' nuclear submarines armed with ballistic missiles were spotted at the open sea area within two hundred nautical miles from the edge of the territorial sea of Accastle. Mercales' current acts of exertion of their claims of sovereignty over the said area include exploiting the natural resources there and building a *man-made island* in that part of the Atlantic Ocean. Mercales demarcates the contested area as its own, based on historic evidence of seafaring by Mercales' admirals," reported the male newscaster on the television.

Widening her round sage-green eyes while drying her soft-layered medium bob hair and shaking her head in disapprobation, Elsie grimaced at the tough luck of Accastle in getting a terrible southern neighbour like Mercales, with only a thin stretch of sea between them. *Looks like the legend of Accastle, the accursed land created from the corpses of millions of demons, is not going to keep the greedy grubber from eyeing our sea.*

However, the marine geophysicist, who normally had vast interests in current affairs, was soon distracted by that vivid dream flashing in her mind. Her thoughts were still on it even after she had changed into a white cotton shirtwaist dress and put on a matching cloche with blood-red lace ribbon—as much as she liked hanging around the seaside, she always wore a hat to maintain her alabaster complexion since she was prone to getting freckles. And that strange occurrence lingered on her mind as she stepped out of the three-storey resort to head to the nearest coast—the one where her nightmare had taken place. It was a long trek of more than two kilometres, but it was one that all tourists and villagers alike had to go through to get to the shore. "Too dangerous." That was the reply of all locals when enquired on why there was no building in the vicinity near the sea.

Countless of drowning incidents, strange disappearances, peculiar tidal patterns that could flood great spans of land—that was the other reason for Elsie's choice to spend her holiday there, and urban legends deemed the area around the shoreline to be very unsuitable for residence and sightseeing in the night time. But she was drawn to the mysteries surrounding that place. *Nothing can't be solved by scientific data and evidence. If we look and analyse hard enough, we can find them.*

Then she remembered that nightmare again. *Is subconscious at work here ... but how about the pain?*

As Elsie was walking along the beach, looking at the sand that gathered between her toes and red sandals and thinking of searching the internet to find answers to her questions, she absentmindedly knocked into a youngster standing in front of her, causing him to spill the entire contents in his bottle of sunscreen lotion.

"Hey, watch it," yelled the teenage blond guy in swimming trunks, who seemed to have a streak of troublemaker in him.

What's wrong with me? I'd never been this careless. Elsie repeatedly bobbed her head in an apologetic manner while rummaging through her bag to get her whiteboard.

He sneered in annoyance. "How are you going to pay for it? And at least say a 'sorry' first."

She just held up her hand, silently requesting him to wait.

"Oh, come on. Are you mute?" he shouted into her ears.

Hearing the commotion, a tall, well-built tan man with close-crop bistre-brown hair, donning dark blue surfer board shorts, rushed up to them while lugging his surfboard along. "Hey, what's up?" he questioned in a sonorous voice.

When the surfer dude reached Elsie, he took one hard look at her before turning to the teen. "Cool it, kid. What had she done to warrant the verbal abuses from you?"

"She wants to get away after making this mess"—the young one pointed at the milky puddle at his feet—"and *not* paying for it," he complained.

Elsie shook her head and finally fished out her handy little board.

The dark-haired man retorted in a stern tone, "Still, you're over-reacting."

While the boy was being reprimanded, Elsie wrote on the whiteboard, "Sorry. Will compensate you." Then she showed it to the kid.

As the towering surfer put up an imposing air and stared at the lad in reproach, the youngster hurriedly put out his hand and announced the price of the sunscreen, without inflating the price as he had intended to. After getting a few notes from Elsie while grumbling under his breath, the teenager quickly gathered his belongings, ordered his friends to get a move on and shifted to a location far away to escape the disapproving glare of the man.

Looking at the boy scampering away, the helpful guy grimaced and mumbled, "Kids ... need some training to whip them into shape."

Then he turned to Elsie and flashed a bright broad smile, inducing a blush on the lady's face due to the warmth of that smile—like the sun empowered with the ability to banish all darkness away. The slight dimples near the ends of his lips infused a boyish charm into his jaunty deposition. "Hope your mood is not spoiled by that brat."

Shaking her head, Elsie beamed with gratitude and pulled out her communication board, meant for Augmentative and Alternative Communication. Pinning the whiteboard under her right arm and holding up the communication board, she put her index finger on the one of the printed boxes that read, "Thank You."

Realization manifested in his deep set brown eyes that sparkled like smoky topaz. "Oh ..." Then he ran his fingers through his wet hair, which was slowly drying under the full blaze of the sun, before extending another hand to Elsie. "No problem. Anyway, I'm Kiefer Knight."

Elsie clutched the communication board in her left hand and tried to stretch out her right hand, with the whiteboard still under her arm.

Upon seeing Elsie's awkward movements, the guy quickly offered to hold the whiteboard for her.

She nodded profusely in appreciation of his help and plied off the marker attached to the side of the whiteboard. "Elsie Irvine. Nice to meet you!" she penned down on the board. Her writing was widely spaced with narrow loops and pointed letters.

"Beautiful name," he blurted.

When her eyebrows arched up, he chuckled and explained, "Irvine refers to a Celtic river, right? I always have a liking for the oceans, rivers, lakes ..."—he raised his broad shoulders—"you know."

Parting her lips slightly in surprise, Elsie immediately scribbled, "So do I." She pointed at herself before turning her communication board around to bring his attention to the handwritten words "Marine Geophysicist" on the back.

His jaws dropped open. "Wow, that's amazing. Outdoors or indoors?"

She replied with the word "indoor" jotted down on her whiteboard. *For obvious reasons. I don't need to talk to computers while doing modelling and calculations to understand the seafloor and sub-seafloor geology....*

Then she wondered if his job was related to water also, thus she widened her eyes and pointed at him as indications to enquire on his occupation.

Planting his hands on his hips, he declared with pride, "Navy lieutenant, just back from active duty. Will go out to the seas of Accastle to protect our territorial waters in two weeks' time."

Looking at Kiefer with admiration, she proceeded to put in writing her thoughts. *I've huge respect for your guys. Not easy job. Especially with the ongoing conflict with Mercales.*

The man grimaced in indignation. "Yes. And the pacifist stance of our government is not helping. They got to realize it's not going to work on rogue countries like Mercales." After letting out a sigh, he shrugged. "Still got to give our best. For this country, for our families and friends."

Elsie made an earnest nod in agreement. Just then she took note of the tattoo on his left chest. *This willingness to sacrifice himself for his love.*

Noticing Elsie's eyes were on his chest, Kiefer coolly informed, "This is from the song 'Hallowed Be Thy Name' by *Indecision*"—then he put up his index finger for emphasis—"but I don't agree with the lyrics that come after this."

When she appeared to be puzzled, tilting her head to the side, he answered with a musing expression, "It's about *not* sacrificing for those that one has never seen. As a personnel in the navy, I should strive to protect all citizens of Accastle. Strangers or not." Then a thought struck him. "Talking about strangers. Are you a tourist here? Since I'd never seen you before."

The lady bobbed her head and tapped the communication board to query if he was a local there.

"Yes, a proud son of Bantora Village." His eyes began to shine with excitement when he suggested, "I can be your personal tour guide. Sanctuary for rare native birds, waterfalls, markets and the best view of Atlantic Ocean from the top of a limestone cliff. And don't worry, it's free of charge."

Sure? She regarded him with surprise and then threw a glance at his surfboard. *Won't it interrupt your planned activities?*

The carefree-looking guy laughed and waved his hand. "I can continue my surfing on another day. No hassle there. Besides, this is a good chance to show the famed community spirit of Bantora."

Hugging her boards close to her chest, Elsie dipped her head as gesture of consent. While she originally wanted to spend her entire holiday looking at the sea only, she did find the thought of a suave guy like Kiefer accompanying her to be somewhat inviting. And she did not regret her decision. Her tour guide of the day was surprisingly attentive, reacting promptly to cues that hinted at her thoughts. His agility and great strength proved to be vital when scaling a pretty steep slope to get to the top of the cliff. He always had a strong grip on her wrist, never letting go once until Elsie had steadied her footing on the plateau. His hold on her somehow made her felt that she was in good hands.

Though to Elsie, the best part of the tour were the conversations she had with Kiefer. His adventures, his heroic deeds, the bonding with his brothers-in-arms, the goofy things they did to stay strong amid the harsh environments and the stand-offs with hostile forces encountered, Elsie took them all in with gusto. Kiefer's world was one that she would never have the chance to experience. But she could imagine herself living through it when listening to Kiefer talking animatedly about his time of service.

Even though Elsie was eager to hear more about the lieutenant's life when out on the seas, Kiefer liked to pepper his talks with questions on her instead. He paid absolute attention to her when she wrote, moved her hands and fingers, and pointed at the communication board to express herself. Nothing else could distract him from his companion, not the passes made at him by the other ladies, nor the daring female tourists who were stripping to get the full effects of the sun tanning.

And their chats always managed to lead to discussions on the tense situation between Accastle and Mercales. Kiefer seemed visibly impressed by Elsie's knowledge on the matter, and the fondness lingering in his eyes swelled with every minute he gazed at her.

When the sun was sliding to the other end of the world to cast her sunlight, Kiefer insisted on accompanying Elsie back to her resort in spite of her initial rejection. "Too dangerous," he reminded. And the signs of worry were evident on his face. His usual jovial demeanour suddenly morphed into one of absolute seriousness.

Elsie was naturally bemused and curious about his words and the change in his mood. However, the guy seemed more interested in getting her home than engaging in talks about the past and supernatural realms.

The moment they reached the main entrance of her resort, Kiefer requested with grave sobriety, "I'm sure the guys here had been telling you this, but still, I need to say it: don't venture out of here at night."

Elsie smiled in appreciation of his advice and pointed at the words "Thank You" on her board.

After they parted ways, with a bit of reluctance, especially on Kiefer's side, Elsie made her way back to her room to get a quick shower. After refreshing herself, she put on a pastel blue cotton house dress and proceeded to amble out of the resort's premises and towards the coastline.

Despite all the warnings, Elsie craved to spend some time alone, looking at the sea, with no crowd, no chatters, no jostling, not caring how the world looked at her. She felt as if she was in control of everything when she had all of the seemingly boundless body of water to herself. There was nowhere else in urban civilizations where such desolated beach existed, except in Bantora Village. And Elsie refused to be deterred by the foreshadowed dangers and let pass the rare chances of indulging in the solitary of infinity.

I didn't encounter anything out of ordinary anyway.

She headed straight to her usual spot, where she had been hanging around for the past few nights: a flat rock outcrop in the shape of a blunt arrow seeking to pierce through the sea. The eerily quiet beach mantled in the claws of the night was a stark contrast from its vibrant and lively counterpart bathed in the sunlight. After carefully trod down a gentle rocky slope and then settling down on the edge of the outcrop, she snuggled into the embrace of the cool gentle breeze saturated with the smell of the ocean. As the wind brushed against her skin, a rush of tunes gracefully spiralled into her mind, and she began to whistle them, hoping that besides the foamy waves: her only audience, the lifeforms in the sea could also hear her songs and dance to them.

Just as the lady was on her tenth song, she saw from afar, tens of metres away, the silhouette of a man half-submerged in the water. Through the dwindling rays of the sun reflecting off his skin that seemed to be glazed with a thin layer of silver varnish, she could see the rippling muscles and defined contours of his shoulders, arms and the sides of his torso. With his back to the sun, his face was encased in a darkness that was as engulfing black as his long straight hair.

Holding her breath, Elsie froze for a second, then lunged forward and squinted her eyes to confirm if what she had just sighted was mere illusion. But the mysterious being dived down to the depths of the ocean. Elsie could only catch a fleeting glimpse of the blade-like caudal fin resembling that of a great white shark before he disappeared into the sea.

Chapter 2 Ghosts

Riding on the metres-high waves, Kiefer was the epitome of sheer focus as he maintained his balance on the surfboard. A minute misjudgement was all it took to break up the sync between the man and the waves to send him plummeting into the blue ocean.

Clutching the rim of her derby hat to prevent the wind from snatching it away, Elsie was sitting on the bed of sand and watching on in awe of the guy's agility and athletic ability to keep up with the ever-changing landscape of churning currents. While the lady had no interest in outdoor sports of any kind since she was afraid of getting tan and her interest lay in Mathematics and Geography, she, surprisingly, enjoyed seeing Kiefer dominating the waves. *It just feels different when I know the person. To be able to cheer for him because I truly care....*

Just then, Kiefer threw a glance at Elsie and ended up tumbling into the sea. When he emerged from the frothing waves few seconds later, Elsie's heart skipped. Not only because the soaking wet topless man with buff physique strolling against the backdrop of raging water was a sight to behold, it also reminded her of that enigmatic entity she saw last night. The guy quickly grabbed his surfboard before it drifted away. Then he jogged to Elsie, who smiled at him to imply that she was impressed. The sunny vibe around him became brighter at her smile.

After the energetic Kiefer parked himself right beside Elsie, splashing some sand in the process, he announced, "Lasted longer than the previous round. Aw man, the waves are sure in a bad mood today. They show no mercy in thrashing us up real bad."

Elsie immediately scribbled out her thoughts. *Still, you'd conquered them. That's very impressive already.*

"Yes, conquer ..." he murmured while staring at the sea with a wistful look.

The curious Elsie leaned forward and turned to study his face, trying to figure out what was on his mind.

Upon realizing that the lady was regarding him with puzzlement, he quickly nudged his mind out of the sea of past and shook his head to clear his mind. Then his lips formed a somewhat melancholic smile. "Yes, conquer the waves, conquer the sea and conquer my fear.... I'd come a long way since my close brush with death"—he pointed at the beautiful, clear dark blue waters of the ocean—"right in there."

Instinctively, Elsie scrawled on the whiteboard the dreaded name "Ioteidas" and ended it with a question mark.

With his eyes on the whiteboard, he lifted his shoulders. "That creature of the legend sounds unreal. There's no sighting of it since it was killed, as said in that myth. Maybe it's sleeping somewhere deep in the ocean, recovering from the wounds and biding its time to strike again. As one of the hideous minions mass slaughtering humans and threatening to push mankind to extinction in olden times, it may have the resilience to survive the wounds inflicted by humans."

Intrigued, she put up her three fingers. *You're talking about the legend of the three heavenly warriors defeating the evil demonic forces and creating the land of Accastle from their corpses, right?*

He nodded. "Yes. *But* the real dangers lurking in this village are the ghosts. The old dudes and ladies here will say that those are the apparitions of the people drowned in the sea. Due to the fluid nature of water, they're trapped in there. They lure people to death in the continuous, hopeless pursuit for a body, just so they can walk the land again."

The wide-eyed lady, with her face frozen in horror fascination, did not move a single muscle, listening intently to Kiefer.

Drawing a deep breath, he went on to divulge, "I lost my mother when I was eight. She went out one night and never returned. Her slippers were found on the beach.... I missed her. I didn't believe she was gone."

Elsie placed a hand on his forearm in hopes of offering some comfort to him.

He smiled in response. "Thanks. You know, there was this one night, I had this impulse to look for her. Without the old man's knowledge, I slipped out of my house. Then I heard my mother calling for me. I ran all the way to the beach and saw her standing over the sea. But ..."

He swallowed a gulp of air before continuing, "When my feet touched the water, she changed into a mass of ghosts that pulled me into the sea. The old man, erm, I mean my dad, and Brandon got there in time to grab a hold on me before I disappeared into the sea. They kept on yanking me towards the dry land while the young Gavin was huddling against the old man and asking for God's help. And so ... here I am." The guy resumed his cheerful disposition and looked grateful to be alive after such ordeal.

Quickly displaying her communication board, Elsie pointed at Kiefer before tapping the words "Awesome guys" on the board.

Appearing to be bashful at Elsie's compliments, he blurted, "I have an awesome family." Then an idea hit him, and his eyes brightened with eagerness as he proposed, "Hey, how about checking out the old man's shop tomorrow? You may find some great souvenirs to bring home.'

She bobbed her head enthusiastically. *Sure.* She was eager to meet the man who could surpass all odds to raise his three sons to such fine young chaps.

***

Elsie admired the eerie beauty of the bone-white, unnaturally huge and round moon that was suspended in the rufescent sky. However, even that seemingly demonic light shed by the moon failed to cut through the opacity of the dark sea, only dancing across the surface of the turbulent currents. After whistling for an hour—far longer than usual, there was still no sight of the sphinx-like being she had spotted the night before. Feeling a bit downcast, she began to wonder if the man was just a figment of her imagination arose from the desire to have an audience listening to her.

Time to head back to the resort.

Getting ready to set off, she took one hard look at sea before leaving. There was nothing outré in sight.

The slightly disappointed lady got up and proceeded to gingerly climb down the rocky platform. Upon touching down on the sand, she dangled her scandals from her curled fingers and walked listlessly down the shore, feeling the fine sand crunching beneath her feet.

A gigantic splash of water in a distance broke the rhythm of the slushing of the undisturbed yet relentlessly strong waves.

Shocked, she whirled around and strained her eyes to try to catch a glimpse of who ... or what had made that splash.

More splashes followed, and the proximity of each subsequent one to her was getting closer. As if an unknown entity was inviting her into the impenetrable abyss of the sea. Enthralled by the strange occurrence, she was drawn into a trance, unknowingly walking towards the interface between the safe haven of the solid land and the dangerous depths of the formless sea.

"They lure people to death in the continuous, hopeless pursuit for a body, just so they can walk the land again."

Kiefer's words jolted Elsie back to reality, and she immediately stopped in her tracks just before the water enveloped her toes. Feeling the dampness of the sand soaked with seawater, she quickly hopped two steps back. With her eyes fixated on the receding waves, she was breathing heavily and thanking her lucky stars that she came to her senses fast enough to escape the fate of being gobbled up by the sea.

Those warnings hold some truth after all.... That was close.

Bony, spectral hands suddenly burst out from the approaching roll of sea foams and sank their claws into Elsie's feet and ankles, burning her skin with their icy cold touch and dragging her into their grave.

Caught off-guard, Elsie crashed down onto the floor, and then her body was hauled across the sand to carve a shallow trench in it. Her desperate clawing at the soft, powdery sand did little to halt her descend to the awaiting dimension of limbo.

Help! Help me!

The next moment, she plunged into the incredibly cold water. In there, dozens of twisted faces of the tormented souls appeared before her, illuminating the increasingly tenebrous surroundings. They were grinning in delight at the prospect of possessing her body, thus freeing themselves from the shackles of the watery prison. Yet their distorted features made them looked like they were shrieking in unbearable pain, contradicting with their blood-curdling, sharp laughter that pierced through Elsie's eardrums.

Holding her breath, she tried to swim towards the moon that was shining brightly above her. However, the glowing globe was getting smaller with each passing moment. And hopelessness was filling up her very psyche as water poured into her lungs. The pain in her chest and lungs was excruciating, but she could do nothing except to begrudgingly join those ghosts to live through their endless nightmares.

Without warning, the faces in front of her, one by one, exploded into wisps of ghostly matter before slowly reconstituting back to their previous forms. Their screams of joy mutated into those of pure horror. Despite losing the strength to focus on anything, Elsie could not help staring in morbid fascination at how the unholy, seemingly untouchable wraiths were being blighted repeatedly as they tried to become whole again.

Through the chaos, she saw a man torpedoing towards her from great distance away, like an unstoppable bullet zipping through the water.

It's him.

Within a few seconds, he came within her reach. Notwithstanding the great speed the man was travelling at, he effortlessly whooshed to a sudden stop, right in front of her as he wanted to.

The sudden rush of opposing currents sent his waist-length, sleek, lustrous, raven-black hair swirling around him, like a mesmerizing billow of unnaturally dark, fine smoke framing his exquisite oval-shaped face. His heavy-lidded eyes, with long, lush eyelashes perched on the edges of his eyelids, looked like beautiful, crystal-clear, aqua blue indicolite gems whose rims were tainted black by the intangible pain and sorrow infesting his soul.

Though captivated by his ethereal eyes, Elsie broke the eye contact as she convulsed and shrivelled due to the pain in her lungs. When her eyes were on his body, she noticed that his smooth silver-tinted human-like skin around his belly button and his defined external oblique muscles at the hips, when going further down, gradually became coarse shark skin covered with dermal denticles. Instead of man's anatomy, he had a lower body of a shark. And there were large gills adorning his torso on where the ribcage was. *No wonder he swims like shark.*

However, the shock of the discovery was displaced by the fear of impending doom as her life-force seeped out of her.

Moving up to Elsie, the mysterious man went on to wrap his arm around her waist and grab her chin. She could feel the sharp tips of his onyx-like claws lightly pressing against her neck and jawline. He parted his lips, which were of the colour of black lily, and revealed his pointed canines before cupping his lips over hers.

What? Before her mind could register anything, his breath rushed into her system to occupy her lungs, pulverizing the water inside and allowing her to breathe ... underwater. As those ghosts scattered away, she realized that she could still see in the darkness, as if through a veil that irradiated the surroundings with cobalt-blue light. Her whole body was infused with a strange warmth, driving out the coldness and melting the very core of her being to meld it with his. She went weak in spite of the life returning to her body.

Then he pulled away from the stunned lady and regarded her intently, with a certain intrigue, before wrapping another arm around her. Looking up at the moon, he shot towards it, holding Elsie firmly in his strong arms and not loosening his grips once while opposing the weight of the massive body of water above them.

Terrified of plummeting into the bottomless chasm below, Elsie snapped shut her eyes and threw her arms around his broad shoulders. After what seemed like an eternity to her, where the rush of water had been scraping against her delicate skin, cool, gentle breeze welcomed her when the two broke out of the surface of the ocean.

But the traumatized lady refused to let go of her sole pillar of hope. Burying her face in his shoulder, pressing her body against his, shivering non-stop and having erratic breathing, she relished the warmth radiated by the merman—not as warm as that of a human, but enough to keep the chill of the wind and water at bay.

Feeling the intense fear in her, the man assured in a deep voice, which was laced with a haunting quality, "Fret not. Those lost souls of the sea dare not touch you again. Though do not trespass into this place during the time when the shadows rule."

She shook her head and interlocked her fingers to ensure that he could not ply her away.

Looking at her in disbelief, he quipped, "That's unnecessary. I'll not let go until I've escorted you back to your world. Hold on."

When Elsie lifted up her head to glance at him and reaffirm what he had said, a billow of water towered over them. That curtain-like wave smacked the sea surface behind the man, creating consecutive waves to push him and Elsie towards the coast. She had the impression that she was just floating on the surface and gently, yet swiftly moving across sea until her feet touched the solid surface of the shore. Taken aback by the somewhat non-existent transportation back to land, she slackened her hold on him.

Then he glided backward, easing himself out of her embrace. She watched him drifting further away as the tide rapidly subsided to ankle level and observed his lips curling up to form a slight smile. Somehow, she could not shake off the feeling that his smile was laden with longing and loneliness.

Chapter 3 Resolve

Lugging a bagful of random items gotten during her "shopping spree" and stepping into the tiny, cosy, rustic, air-conditioned space, accompanied by Kiefer, the astounded Elsie scanned the rows of clay works displayed on the sparsely spaced dark wooden shelves that lined the left and right walls. There were sculptures of the unique, quaint dune shacks—the architectural style of most of the buildings in the village, native flora, fishes and other sea animals. What caught Elsie's eyes were a series of clay figurines portraying a handsome, strong young man, who oddly bore a slight resemblance to Kiefer, wielding a harpoon to fight a hideous amphibious creature in the form of a merman. Saved for the skull shape and torso, the monster looked nothing like a human.

Elsie bent her knees to get a closer look at the figurine in question. Cocking her head, she tried to fathom the reason to the great differences in appearance between the real person and the one in the beliefs. *Are the legends really factually accurate? Or are they twisted according to preferences? Maybe he's really a misunderstood individual, vilified by the rumours borne from fear.*

A fit elderly man in his fifties, wearing silver-rimmed spectacles, baggy jeans and a black pleather jacket over white T-shirt, lumbered out of the art studio through a doorway behind the counter, located at the back of the shop's main area. The loud hammering of his light brown boots against the wooden floor startled Elsie out of her deep thoughts. Smiling at the lady's reactions, the old man, who had full short neat grey hair, remarked, "Welcome to Knight's Crafts. You were looking at a fine specimen unique to Bantora Village. One of a kind that you can't find in anywhere else. Presenting *Ioteidas*! A well-known demon of the sea that preys on humans. Luckily for us, after binging on blood and satisfying its hunger, this creature will sleep for a year before he pops out again to create havoc."

Torn between the urge to correct the shopkeeper on the wrong information and the impulse to chuckle at his candid description, thus Elsie ended up forcing out an awkward smile.

"Hey old man, this *creature* had been sleeping for centuries already," Kiefer pointed out.

Planting his fists on his hips, the shop owner barked as his moustache twitched, "Damn. Look, boy. I'm trying to set up an intriguing setting for that bedtime story, so my customer will be more interested in buying the pieces. Do you have to ruin it for me?"

Kiefer gave him the dead-pan look. "And you spilled the beans right in front of your customer."

Widening his eyes in realization, the older man quickly proceeded to throw open his arms and flash a wide beam at Elsie. "Never mind the usual banters between my clueless son and me. Just know that everything here is fine, quality representations of Bantora Village. Including the mystique surrounding the rich history of this wonderful, humble village left untouched by rapid urbanization. And all are made from natural clay extracted from this area."

Elsie bobbed her head in agreement with his words and showed him the communication board she had on hand before putting her index finger on the "Hello, nice to meet you" square.

"Hello there. Don't be shy. Look around and pick anything you like. These sculptures make great souvenirs and are solid proofs that you've been here," said the elderly Knight.

Kiefer grimaced at his dad's salesman tactics and informed, "She's Elsie."

With his mouth forming an "O", Kiefer's father exclaimed, "Oh, you're the one my boy had been talking about, *happily*, the whole night." He stretched out his hands to grab Elsie's hand and give a firm handshake. "It's a pleasure to have you here. Hi, I'm Chris."

As his face turned red, Kiefer glared at his dad. "You're one hell of a loose cannon."

"And you're a chip off the old block," retorted Chris.

Putting up his thumb and index finger to do a pinching action, Kiefer reminded, "The chip off the *tiny* good part of the block."

Elsie giggled at the "friendly" exchange between the father and son, feeling at ease in the presence of Kiefer's dad, despite her earlier assumptions that he would regard her with pity or subtle hostility.

However, she did not expect Chris to be that friendly when he escorted her to the studio to show off his working space while confining in her, "Growing up without their mum, my boys are hopeless around the ladies. My first kid got his old lady through matchmaking, our great tradition still kept alive until now. And the second one got lucky that a fine lady chased him all the way to the wedding altar. As for my youngest boy, he's good at weaselling out of those matchmaking attempts! And don't be fooled by his tall built. He's a big baby, he has no clue on serenading the lady of his dreams. Heck, he doesn't even know how to confess his affections to her."

Elsie was wondering where the conversation was leading to. She tried to keep a straight face and waited for the big reveal.

Then he exhaled deeply. "So as his old man, I got to give him a hand on this. Elsie, do you—"

"You can try your hand at making a sculpture if you like," shouted Kiefer while barging into the studio.

Chris never had the chance to finish his say. He could only grumble under his breath as his son led Elsie away to a table with wrapped clay bricks stacked on it.

***

Elsie had finished whistling all the songs in her repertoire, but the dark sea remained calm, not a hint of life manifested on the surface, just like the previous night.

Is he avoiding me?

Sighing in disappointment ... and strangely, relief, she stared at her toes half-buried in sand and tried to find a reason to get back to the resort soon.

It's late. Maybe I can start studying those data. Who says you can't work during vacation? I shouldn't get involved with things not of our world anyway.

However, when her eyes followed the gentle movements of the unabated sea currents that fought to reach the shore, only to be dragged back into the sea, Elsie realized that she did not want to leave until she saw him—the monster of the legends. Then she remembered a song that Kiefer had played in his car. It was a melodic metal song that had somehow been woven into her memory in spite of her dislike of the metal genre.

"This song is called 'Yuuki', meaning courage in Japanese."

Within that song, she could distinctly feel the fervour of gathering that courage in oneself. And at that moment, those sentiments slowly diffused from her memory into her pneuma, filling her with a wealth of emotions, which she translated into a tune on her lips. The crisp clear, high-pitched notes fluttered in the air and twirled towards the ocean, bringing with them the wishes of the lady. Lulled into a state of tranquillity, she did not take note of the increasingly agitated movements of the waves. She only realized the folly of her inattention when a giant wave charged at her, ready to devour her.

Quickly standing up and spinning around, but falling down in panic, she went on to squeeze her eyelids shut in preparation for what was to come.

If what he said is true, I'll not be dragged down again. If not, I'll haunt him for his lies.

However, no water pelted down onto her head as expected. She could only feel water rushing up to surround her to her waist level. Opening her eyes with trepidation, she saw her saviour hovering in the sea several metres away from her, with his torso above the water.

Deep ceases gathered between his eyebrows as he snarled, "What do you want? I'd told you this is not the place for you humans to dwell in during the night."

Unwilling to let him slip away again, Elsie hugged the whiteboard and communication board to her chest and sprinted to him, not aware of the giant concave in the beach face just carved by the abnormally huge wave. Then she found herself stepping on nothing solid and dropping down into the ocean.

The beach was not like this in the morning! What sorcery had he wielded? What is he?

As she was completely submerged in the sea, there was violent swirling of the water in front of her. The next second, the man of mystique reached for her by grabbing her upper arms. With those powerful grips of his, he pulled her up to the surface.

While she was quivering from the intense cold and gasping for air, hungry for the oxygen after the lack of it a moment ago, he brought his face nearer to hers and looked on with concern.

Noticing his gaze were fixated on her visage, with the moonlight highlighting his eyes that were saturated with focus, yearning and unfathomable darkness, she blushed. Her awkwardness was compounded by the fact that she was very aware of the strange warmth from his body, his breath rolling off her forehead, and his hands still grasping her arms. And she observed the beads of water streaking down his chiselled features and buff chest that seemed to be dusted with a thin, fine layer of silver varnish. *Good thing he can't see my face properly in the dark.*

"Looks like the colour is returning to your face," he commented, appearing to be ready to send her back to the berm of the beach.

What? He has night vision? Then the images of the sea bathed in cobalt-blue light surfaced onto her mind. The embarrassed lady tried to distract herself by taking out the whiteboard to write her question.

Both her handy little tools of communication were not in her hands and were nowhere to be found.

In her frenzy, she used sign language to communicate her thoughts, not considering if he understood her or not. *Are you the ... demon?* She spelled out the name that most locals feared or hated. *I-O-T-E-I-D-A-S?*

Cocking his head to the side, his eyes clouded by an uncanny serenity and resignation, he replied, "Yes. But your bunch have been lucky that I'd chosen to sleep for the past five centuries. The need to feed has thus been staved off ... for the time being." Then a sliver of primitive hunger and lust flashed across his eyes.

Whether it was due to the surprise at him knowing sign language, or the apprehension of him unshackling his demonic tendencies, a chill spiralled down her spine. She moved her hands and fingers to ask for his purpose in saving her.

Priming me for future feast, right, she mentally answered her own question.

"Your songs ..." He stared out at the landscape behind her, seemingly lost in his own world. "They soothe my pain. Those incessant noises of destruction and death—the results of man's greed ... I was at my breaking point. A dozen will not be sufficient if I start to feed on blood after starving myself for such long time ... to the point I'd forgotten its taste."

A person without a voice ... and yet my songs can do so much? Touched by his words, Elsie wished she could stay around longer to help him and the villagers who were in danger of becoming his victims. There was no fear, only empathy, curiosity and an unexplainable desire dominated her heart. Unknowingly lifting up her hand, she wanted to touch his cheek and allay his pain that was evident in his eyes.

With lightning fast reaction, he caught hold of her wrist, halting her from proceeding further. "Don't. This is the punishment I deserve for defying my fate. It'll be easier if I let go of the guilt and embrace my ineluctable destiny."

Her jaws dropped open at his ability to know what she was thinking. *He can read minds?*

Still clutching her wrist, he smiled coldly at her expression of bewilderment. "I can read faces. The knowledge, the emotions and the thoughts of humans—the winds and the waters carry them to my abode and stamp them into my dreams ... or nightmares."

Such great burdens to shoulder, thought Elsie. She shuddered at the thought of the mental assaults bombarding him even when he wanted to shut himself off from the world. *Is it me who had awakened him?*

"Let me help you to alleviate the pain," she made clear her intention through hand signals.

He chuckled and let go of her wrist. "What can you do? You're just a human. It's for the best that you flee away from this place before the inevitable comes. You'll not be spared when the beast is unleashed."

Something in her snapped. And with her face contorted by a scowl, she straight out told him with unbridled indignation and hardened resolve that nothing was deemed impossible for her. She even threw in a promise that she would make him ate his words. *I'd gotten through so many obstacles in life, what's this challenge to me?*

A corner of his lips twisted up as the sardonic, visibly amused man studied her expressions with interest. "We should see. Perhaps saving you will be the best deed I'd ever done."

Chapter 4 Beauty

After spending the whole night surfing the internet for pain alleviation methods, Elsie was absolutely bummed out by the time the first rays of the sun peeked through the horizon on the east. Tiredness rendered her brain unable to process any information properly. Everything she saw on the screen just skimmed across the surface of her mind without etching into it. She mentally scolded herself for letting the zeal for achieving her aim got over her head, thus failing to exercise self-control and wait until morning to do her "research". Knowing that sleep was needed to clear her muddled head, she stumbled to her bed and then just crashed into it.

"Let me go! Somebody help me!"

Left alone by the sea and handcuffed to the blood-stained boulder, she tried to yank her hands out of the rusted metal cuffs. The violent jerking of her arms caused the metal to cut through her skin and eat into her flesh. However, the fear for her life superseded that pain, pushing her to continue the futile struggle to escape. Her will to fight was strong, but her strength was draining out, along with the blood streaming out of the cuts carved onto her limbs by the elders.

"The demon will seek for the source after catching the scent of blood."

She had no idea how much time had passed when a tremor rumbled through the land she was standing on. At that very moment, every blood cell of hers froze up.

It's coming.

A hollow, hoarse shriek perforated the humid air before a bundle of seething water formed at the surface of the ocean and began to bulldoze its way to the sacrifice.

Elsie was tugged out of the brief stint in the realm of dreams by the ringing of her mobile phone. Before she could gather the strength to get up and get the phone, silence once again permeated the atmosphere in the dark room whose curtains were drawn to block out the sunlight. Though affrighted by the nightmare, she heaved a sigh of relief that it ended before Ioteidas appeared. Somehow, she was scared of seeing him succumbing to his bloodthirst, even in the dreams.

Will I still have that ardent wish to help him if he's really the monster as described?

She began to recall his touches, the tenderness of his dark lips, his strong embraces and the warmth tempered with an almost undetectable shred of humanity lingering in his unworldly eyes when he gazed at her. Her lips parted, and a strange concoction of tingling sensations and numbness washed over them.

He's not a demon ... he's not. I'll find a cure for him to get rid of the thirst for blood.

After sorting out her thoughts, she finally found the strength to get off the bed and check her phone. And she got a surprise when seeing several messages and five missed calls from Kiefer. *Is there a point in calling me?*

Then frantic knocking on her door caused her to jump and drop the phone.

"Elsie, are you in there? Are you okay?" yelled a man standing outside her room.

Realizing that it was Kiefer, Elsie hurriedly smoothed her hair and dress before trotting to the door to open it.

The second the door was swung open, the apparently worried Kiefer lunged forward and hugged Elsie. "I'm so glad to see you're okay. I swear I'll hunt down the culprits and kill them if you're hurt in any way. Be it the ghosts, the shadows or Ioteidas."

Stunned by Kiefer's actions, Elsie stood still like a statue for few seconds. When she recovered from the shock, she patted his back to thank him for his concerns and assure the guy that she was alright.

The light pats seemed to slap him back into reality as he suddenly pulled away from the lady.

She then looked at him in the eyes questioningly.

Rubbing the nape of his neck, the lad had uneasiness scribbled into his peepers when he blurted, "Erm ... you know ... as your tour guide, it's my duty to ensure your safety."

She smiled brightly in response. And without thinking, she made the hand sign that said, "Thanks."

She had learnt from the numerous encounters with great guys that they were nice to her due to political correctness or the perceived need to specially take care of her. No romantic feelings had ever being involved. Thus she understood that Kiefer did what he did because of the wonderful platonic relationship between them. *Don't assume too much....*

***

After settling down on the rock outcrop, her favourite haunt, which Elsie figured to be the most stable place to stay put at, she adjusted the volume of her handphone to the maximum. She went on to open the *Recording* app before inhaling deeply and tapping the "play" button.

Hope this works, and we can call it a day. I'd seen it all, been through it all. Anything that can happen will not ruffle my feathers one bit. It'll be an uneventful day.

The recorded form of her whistling tiptoed out of the speaker of the phone to dance with the evening breeze and transmit Elsie's message to the one residing in the deepest part of the spawning ocean.

The second song hardly started when a breaker smashed against the rocks Elsie was sitting on and drenched the skirt of her polo dress. Then Ioteidas emerged from the sea beside her, face up first. The water brushed his dark, long hair to the back. With his eyes half-closed, he parted his lips and took his first breath of air, indulging in unrestricted access to the much needed oxygen. Elsie observed every move of his and felt a tinge of desire tunnelling through her blood.

Then looking unimpressed, he asserted, "These are just noises. They carry nothing, and they do nothing for me. Your method fails. Be gone now."

Despite her apparent disappointment, she quickly shook her head and signalled to him that she had other tricks up her sleeve. Carefully treading over to the edge of the outcrop, with the water rising up to her knees, and then sitting down with her legs hanging over the rocks, sort of, as they were immersed in water, she proceeded to fish out a tiny glass bottle of lavender essential oil. *This will help you to relax and ease the pain.*

Crinkling his nose in revulsion, he snatched the bottle and tossed it far away—not into the sea, of course. "The so-called aroma is too strong and offensive to my liking."

All of a sudden, his brows gathered together as he clenched his teeth. "They still refuse to spare the ocean of the pillage even in the night. You humans are truly persistent when self-interests are involved," he hissed through ragged breaths, with the repugnance raging in his eyes.

Is it the pain? She sighed softly and brought forth her motto to harden her resolve. *Time for next idea....*

"Acupuncture helps," she informed through hand signs.

Appearing to be sceptical and slightly irritated, he riposted, "I can't guarantee the acupuncturist's safety." Then reaching out to cradle her cheeks and demand her undivided attention, he stared into her eyes. "You do realize you're the only one who can get away unscathed after encounters with me, don't you? I avoid humans for good reasons." A soft deep guttural manifested in his voice at the last sentence.

Startled by his outburst and harsh tone, and unsure of what those entailed, she froze in shock, trying to figure out her next course of action. *Don't tell me this triggers his beastly side to come out.*

Feeling the subtle quivering of her body through his fingertips—a sensation that seemed alien after years of eschewing contact with humans and any being that could communicate with him, he revelled in it and realized he craved to see Elsie again and look into her large expressive eyes in order to feel her rich emotions. Unconsciously, the man ran his thumb over her lips, gliding his sharp nail across the delicate surface of her upper lip. His head inched closer to her. He sought to have a taste of her lips, for the sole purpose of assuaging his wants.

The lady knew what he was going to do, and she was torn between resisting his advances and giving in to her instincts. *This progresses too fast, isn't it?*

He suddenly halted in his tracks and began to tremble, as if he was desperately suppressing the urge to abandon himself to carnal pleasures. Clenching his fists and snapping shut his eyes, he reluctantly let go of her.

At that moment, Elsie wanted nothing more than to be there for the man and help him. Attempting to calm the turmoil within him, she gulped down a mouthful of air before holding a hand of his in her dainty ones and ordering him to close his eyes and think of a peaceful, relaxing scene.

As his muscles slowly relaxed, he smiled at her efforts while challenging, "Why do I need to think of that when I'm right here?"

Shrugging, she positioned her index and middle fingers before her eye and then pointed them outward to tell him to look. She went on to make forward wave motions with her hands to represent the sea.

Appearing to be unconvinced, he did as told by whirling around to face the ocean.

The sun's last flickers of dazzling radiance were scattered across the surface of the ocean, and the path to her was illuminated and rendered gold on the canvas of swirling dark lazulite-blue waves. Before retreating into the ocean, she painted on the bluish-white shimmering sky streaks of champagne gold and coral pink that intertwined with the wisps of clouds. The sky looked like a beautiful moonstone at that moment. The combers of the sea bade farewell to the sun with their rustling, rhythmic melodies.

"It's breath-taking. I never notice despite dwelling in the sea for so long," he breathed.

Elsie nodded eagerly, not taking her eyes off the picturesque ocean. Enthralled by the beauty before her, she began to whistle, proclaiming her love for it.

Ioteidas turned to regard her with endearment. But Elsie did not notice, for she was too engrossed in singing her songs.

When she finished all the tunes that her mind could come up with, both of them did not talk, soaking in the strangely soothing silence and the approaching darkness around them. As minutes ticked by, the lady was slowly becoming aware of the deep inhales and exhales of the merman. She could not help observing the way the gills on his torso moved in sync with his chest.

Noting what she was focusing on, he replied, "You remind me of what I am, and the reason to my existence. It's a matter of time I need to fulfil my obligations, and it will bring fresh pain and unlock demons of the past."

Pressing her lips together, she immediately made clear her opinion. *I'm sure there're ways to circumvent it.*

His response was a twisted smile of cynicism.

Gritting her teeth, and with determination lining her face, she repeated her mantra through sign language. *I'd seen it all, been through it all. So I know nothing is impossible.*

"Seen it all? How about the recesses hidden deep within the ocean?" he questioned.

Not backing down, she made the signs for "T" and "V".

He laughed. "How about the part on 'been through it all'?"

She was stuck dumbfounded for a second. Just as the flustered woman was going to shoot back that she could experience it through her dreams, he put out his hand to her.

"I can take you there," he proffered, looking at her in the eyes, drawing her in.

There's no ocean trench in this part of the Atlantic Ocean. Don't try to fool me. Or is it hidden from us? Seeing the hadalpelagic depth of the ocean.... She began to feel hyped up about his offer.

A second of cogitation caused him to suddenly hesitate, but she had already caught hold of his outstretched hand and took a plunge into sea. The unforgiving coldness immediately seeped into her skin to purge out the warmth within her. However, as the merman yanked her close, the invading, freezing elements were driven out of her.

"Stay close to me," he reminded.

Blushing, she dipped her head and put her arms around his neck to get a secure hold on him.

With the lady in his arms, he glided backward, away from the coast, and followed up with a swivel in the middle of the sea.

With his body in tight contact with hers, feeling the swirls of water encircling her and brushing against her skin, she was like waltzing in the dense, moist air as she twirled and swayed in the water with him. Exhilarating and sensual, it was as if they were dancing to the prelude to the mating ritual. If she had a voice, the air would be filled with coy, soft laughter.

Seeing the lady getting lost in the moment, he gazed at her intently, yearning to just take her. Shoving his amorous thoughts aside, he pressed his lips against hers.

Before Elsie could acknowledge his action and the changes happening in her body, the man pulled her down into the domain ruled by him.

Once underwater and getting accustomed to the fact that she could breathe in there, Elsie gasped at the splendour and magnificence of the crystal blue world obscured from most land dwellers. A school of Atlantic herrings were swimming in the same direction, at the same speed and in an almost choreographed manner. The school was like a fine transparent veil embellished with ornate silver embroidery curling and weaving through the sea. Luxuriating in a world of their own, those fishes swam without a care for anything else, except for the dance of their clan.

The two's journey continued as Ioteidas held onto Elsie's hand and guided her to another part of the ocean. The grand presence and imposing size of the somewhat warm-blooded apex predator, the Atlantic Bluefin tuna, who moved gracefully through the water by using its enormous muscular strength for propulsion, the myriad of brilliantly coloured—sunshine yellow, electricity blue, rose pink, pumpkin orange, emerald green—corals that flaunted their dazzling beauty, the tiny, energetic fishes that darted around the maze of corals where millions of lives flourished in, the majestic manta ray idly flapped its wing-like pectoral fins to soar through the sea, the antiquity of the tenacious European sea sturgeon that had traversed between the ocean and rivers, and the oddity of the jellyfishes warbling in the water—all spellbound Elsie to no ends.

When the two went further down southwest, they were greeted by a pod of Atlantic spotted dolphins who came in great variations of colourings: mottled, fused, speckled and two-tone. Upon sensing the friendly vibe of Elsie, those curious cetaceans assembled around the woman to observe her. The touched lady stared in awe at the rare sight of dolphins gathering before her, as if they understood that she was there to connect with them.

After few seconds ticked by, the dolphins proceeded to playfully swim around Elsie and Ioteidas while whistling and clicking. Reaching out, she ran her hands affectionately over the smooth, rubbery skin of their backs whenever those lovely creatures zipped past her.

As for the man, he watched on in admiration of Elsie's generous showering of care onto those sea mammals and her effortless interactions with them.

She would have easily spent an hour or two frolicking with the dolphins. However, the night was short, and Ioteidas signalled to her to move on to the deeper part of the ocean. Therefore, she could only begrudgingly bid farewell to her new friends.

Then came the sharks, sliding through the waters with speed, grace and precision. She froze in trepidation as childhood horror stories flooded her mind. But the man beside her remained calm and made no attempt to get her out of there.

The three Selachimorpha just swam close by and around the merman and his companion once before perambulating to another far corner of the boundless ocean. Elsie almost laughed her own momentary ignorance as she watched them disappear from her sight. Ioteidas smiled slightly and gently guided her off to where the unknowns of the sea hid.

As they dived deeper into the sea, the vibrancy diminished, and the peculiar creatures thriving in the blanketing darkness of the abyssopelagic depths of the ocean were of anomalous appearances seen only in the wildest, most bizarre imaginations. In fact, if not for Ioteidas' energy running through her system, Elsie would only be able to see immeasurable void of infinity and nothing, and her body would be crushed by the incredible water pressure.

As the fear of the unknowns burrowed its way into her heart, she moved her hands and fingers to ask him the question lingering on her mind. *Is this where you reside at?*

His face was devoid of emotions when he held up his fist to move it up and down to give her the affirmative answer in sign language. Though an almost undetectable frown betrayed his hidden, dark thoughts.

How can anyone live here for so long without losing his sanity? It's too empty, too dark, too depressing. Even the unsociable lady found it unbearable.

Biting her lower lip, she tried to stop her emotions from overwhelming her, but the tears gushed out of her eyes anyway. *He'll not see the tears with all the water around anyway.*

Her reddened peepers and lugubrious expressions could not escape his eyes. He stopped in his tracks, signalled that they were going up and proceeded to wrap his arms around her and head for the shore.

After they broke out of the water surface and took in big gulps of air, Ioteidas studied Elsie's visage while trailing his fingers along her jawline and saying under his breath, "I shouldn't have brought you down there. Why do I always lose myself when with you?"

Placing a hand on his chest, over the heart, Elsie was hoping that he could sense what she was thinking. *Sadness is part of life. This is part of the route to understand you. I've no complaints nor regrets. I truly want to explore your world again ... no, umpteen times.*

The visibly touched man put his hand over hers and then curled his fingers to clasp her hand tightly.

Chapter 5 Secret

Perching on the carpet of lush, sea-green wild grasses at the top of the cliff with Kiefer, and surrounded by exuberant foliage and patches of scurvy grass, blooming sea pink and sheeps bit—floras that survived on thin soils and stood against the strong gales, Elsie watched from afar the ships and boats sailing towards the port at the southern tip of Accastle and carefully avoiding the waters around the west. The panoramic view of the ocean from the highest point in Bantora was unparalleled, yet only a handful of people were there. Elsie was feeling lucky that she had Kiefer to bring her there. For the cliff was out-of-bounds to all non-locals, unless they were in the company of residents who were certified to be fit and equipped to scale the slope leading to the cliff. Records of the past had shown that too many accidents had occurred there, and the village could not afford to allow more of such tragedies to happen if it was within their control.

"Have you heard of the story about how this cliff was formed," asked Kiefer, who was lying down, with his hands behind his head, and admiring the fluffs of white cotton-candy-like clouds drifting across the clear cerulean blue sky.

Turning her attention from the sea to Kiefer, Elsie shook her head.

"It's an old story passed down through generations. They said during the battle between the forces of good and evil, one of the heavenly warriors, an Archmage ... he's called Scales or something along that line ... well, he summoned a gigantic tornado"—Kiefer twirled his index finger to resemble a whirlwind—"it went whoosh and sucked in the demons. Tore them into pieces and then compressed the bits into a humongous pillar. And with the bodies piling up beside this pillar, a new landscape was moulded from these." Then he flashed a mischievous grin at Elsie. "Yes, we're resting on that pillar right now. Can you feel that it's alive with"–then his voice took on a deeper tone—"demonic powers?"

She puckered up her lips and playfully smacked his arm. *Stop scaring me. I'm not falling for that. I'd seen it all, been through it all. Slain demons can't be alive.* When the image of Ioteidas came into her mind, she mentally added, *except for one.*

Then she wrote down her immediate thoughts upon hearing the tale before showing Kiefer the word "cruel" on the whiteboard.

Pursing his lips and cocking his head, he went into deep thoughts for a second prior to remarking, "Most of us will not see it that way since they're demons, evil species different from us."

The look of disapproval thundered across Elsie's face. *Provided they have no thoughts and feelings.*

He smiled at Elsie's silent disagreement. "Hey, that's how things are. See how enemies can kill each other on the battlefield without thinking that it's cruel? But I can see where you're coming from. With the escalating tension between Accastle and Mercales, it's a matter of time I engage in crashes with Mercales' vessels. Yeah, there's another news on Mercales' patrol ships spotted around Accastle's waters *again.*"

Elsie frowned at the news. *Our navy needs to bomb the hell out of them.* Then she gasped at the realization that her savage thoughts immediately surfaced at a slight provocation, despite her earlier proclamation against cruelty.

Noticing the lady's reactions, he gave her an assuring look to show that he had the same thoughts. "I can't help thinking that they, too, have families waiting for them to go home. Like that nagging old man waiting for his chances to bark at me when I'm back."

"He has to juggle between the roles of dad and mum," Elsie penned down on the board.

He chuckled at her reply and quipped in a joking manner, "Luckily, he doesn't go literal on these and starts crossdressing to be mum."

Giggling, she made known her thoughts on the whiteboard. *He's a wonderful dad who had raised a bright young man to protect the waters of Accastle and our sovereign rights.*

Ioteidas' words then bolted through her head. "*Rights hold no meaning to me. I only concern myself with who's desecrating my territory. And to make them pay for their crimes with their lives.*"

But what's holding him back from going on a carnage?

Upon seeing Elsie's comments, Kiefer gazed at her intently in the eyes. "I know the old man is worried about me. I want to make him proud of me and at the same time, hoping that I can come back home safely. But I'd never thought about settling down. I'm twenty-five only, so I was like, hey, I'm still young. But now, I'm contemplating my next steps in life. Well ..." Somehow, he could not continue.

As her eyes gleamed with avidity, Elsie excitedly highlighted the phrase "Go for it" on the communication board. *I'm behind you on this.*

***

Elsie marvelled at the mysteries hidden in the nooks and crannies of the seemingly boundless ocean as she and Ioteidas weaved through the narrow space between two cliff-like structures. Despite having explored the ocean for the past three nights, Elsie was still mesmerized and astounded by the unreal beauty of the world submerged in the sea. No amount of scientific data and representations that she had pored over could quantify the experience of being immersed in there. And sign language was like the most natural language to utilize when underwater. The two could "talk" for hours while navigating through the ocean.

Having exhausted all the possible and innovative ways to relieve his headaches, she knew that only her presence and songs could help him in the meantime. However, disaster loomed as the newspaper exploded with reports on Mercales' rampant decimation of the reefs in Atlantic Ocean and that country's fishermen's non-stop, large-scale harvesting of endangered species and fishes in there. As if affected by those acts of savagery committed, the pain he endured was intensifying with each passing day, and he was feeling an increasing urge to respond to his calling. Her searches on the internet yielded nothing on Ioteidas' hunger for blood. *Hydrophobia, porphyria, Renfield's syndrome, anemia ... he doesn't have the symptoms that point to any of these.*

Nevertheless, she tried to think on the bright side. *We can take things one at a time.*

As they ventured deeper into the narrow passage, Elsie noticed the light casted around her getting dimmer, causing her to squint her eyes.

A hesitation in keeping up due to the failing vision, and a light tug on his hand that was clasping hers were all Ioteidas needed to realize that she was not feeling alright. He immediately reached over to cup her chin and give her a puff of his breath to imbue her body with the ability to resist the punishing elements of the sea.

Elsie knew full well that the contact of their lips was just a process in the means to enable her to stay underwater. Never once had he lost control of himself, even though she had spotted fleeting flashes of primitive lust whizzing through his eyes. Yet the closeness to him, his touches and the taste of his supple lips incited that deep-seated desire within her. She wanted more. She wanted to be an integrated part of his world. She wanted him to kiss her with passion.

When he pulled away from her, she grabbed his biceps, not firmly, as her hands were too dainty to get a steady hold on his muscular arms. Swimming up to him, she gave him a quick peck on the lips before gathering the courage to run her tongue across his lower lip.

He closed his eyes and stayed motionless, as if he was desperately clinging onto his last shred of control, while she was lightly nipping his lips. It was finally too much for him to take ... and without a warning, he yanked the lady into his tight embrace and reciprocated her show of affection with deep, fervid, consuming kisses that engulfed her entire state of existence. She had never realized how much he wanted her until he ran a hand up her back to grip her shoulder and pull her in, almost crushing the breath out of her, so as to savour the full extent of the kisses.

As the inseparable lovers sealed their bond and indulged in the moment, the water around them swirled and danced to the silent tune of their union.

***

Under the cool early morning sun that was dispersing her rays generously and cheerfully over the shore, Elsie, with a hand pressing on the crown of her cloche, walked along the beach, looked at the sea and wondered if Ioteidas would burst out of there when she started whistling.

"I've no aversion towards sunlight." That was his answer when she had asked him if he appeared during night-time only.

Still, it's better to let him sleeps through the peak of the pain as he wants. Sleep helps to dull the pain, I guess.

Elsie pondered about how long he could take the ever increasing frequency of the occurrences of the headaches, and the pain was exacerbated with each subsequent one. She wished to be there for him, for her presence could neutralize the pain.

"Call for me with your songs."

Recalling his words, she was tempted to start whistling. Yet the impulse to do so was curbed by the boisterous laughter of a family. Gazing at the kids and their Jack Russell dog chasing after the father down the beach while the mother ambled behind them all, Elsie decided not to endanger their lives. While she believed that Ioteidas was not a cold-blooded monster as said, she shuddered at the prospect of him encountering humans, the very beings he had avoided for centuries.

***

Hidden behind a massive, dense kelp forest, whose tall seaweeds swayed gently with the currents while reaching for the sky, was a crevice on a towering rock formation, just wide enough for a person to slide through. And in it was a dark secret passage that led to an underwater cave. Time seemed to stand still in that mystical world. The fine, powdery sand on the sea floor, left unruffled for years until the arrival of Ioteidas and Elsie, formed a luxurious, velvet-like carpet draping lovingly over the soft curves of the floor. In sharp contrast were the jagged rock ceiling and walls that arched over the entire place. Their coarse, raw, unpolished surface told ancient stories of how Mother Nature shaped the underwater domain. Fauna unknown to humans survived the climatic changes through millions of years and proliferated in that sanctuary.

Within that cave, in a dark corner, lay a cranny just big enough for two lovers to hide in and cosy up with each other. Ioteidas entered that sanctum with Elsie in tow before pulling her into his embrace.

Cut off from the outside, feeling exceptionally safe and protected in their secret hideout, Elsie buried her face in her man's chest, flinging aside all the mundane concerns of the world.

But that feeling of abandonment was short-lived as the inquisitive lady looked up at Ioteidas and commented through hand signals, "Baffling that this cave eludes detection by the most advanced equipment."

Using sign language, he revealed the chilling fact that the ghosts loved to congregate around there, thus creating illusions and making the most advanced equipment malfunctioned. The lack of sunlight amplified their abilities to manipulate their surroundings.

Sounds like they're part of his army. Shuddering at the thought of her near-death encounter with those apparitions, she gazed at the haven before her, trying to catch a glimpse of them floating around in spite of her apprehension to see them again. Then her mind drifted to the idea on how humans could benefit from exploring that secret cavern to make new discoveries in science. Like how the scientists studied the organisms living in the oxygen-depleted underwater caves in Bahamas to look into the possibility of life beyond Earth. Then she gave Ioteidas a look of excitement, like she had stumbled upon a treasure trove.

Putting a finger over her lips, he shook his head before holding up his fist, with the thumb sticking out, to tap the back of that thumb against his dark lips twice.

She immediately understood that the place must remained a secret between them. In fact, deep inside her heart, the selfish side of her wanted it to stay that way. *I'll never tell.*

When he utilized the hand signs to convey his thoughts, the engrossed woman looked intently at him and could imagine him saying, "This is one of the few places left undiscovered and untainted by humans' relentless greed. The time of destruction comes when humans find this hideout and hanker for the so-called treasure hidden here. They'll ravage, pillage and plunder this place, striping it bare of all lifeforms."

His face was notably marked with disdain as he continued, "Humans' hearts will always be bound by the allure of monetary gains instead of the beauty of nature."

"Do you hate humans?" Elsie asked in their silent mode of communication even though she knew the obvious.

"Absolutely" was his answer.

When perplexity was scribbled onto her visage, his expressions softened, and he regarded the confused woman with tenderness while tracing the contours of her facial features and using another hand to tell her, "You're different. Your determination.... Your love for the ocean ... it's woven into your melodies."

Blinking her eyes, the moved lady wanted to confess her desire to be always with him and explore the entirety of his underwater palace. The man smiled warmly and informed her that he would take her to anywhere in the Atlantic Ocean she wished to venture to.

Mildly surprised, Elsie arched up her eyebrows and queried on the possibility of knowing every corner of his vast ocean.

With a cocky look on his face, he nodded once before divulging that the ancient knowledge accumulated did not fade. However, a gloom shrouded his eyes when he added that only the memories of recent times were pulverized.

"Every time I feed and go into deep sleep, some memories will be lost. And I'll morph into a creature that is ... more exalted." Then he tightened his jaws in agony at the loss of pieces of his life. All he remembered of them was that they were of tantamount importance.

The concerned lady clasped his hand to give him assurance and bring comfort to his tormented psyche.

When he relaxed at her touch, she put her right index finger over her mouth, followed by the action of pressing her right palm against the thumb side of her left clenched fist. She went on to fold down her right thumb and use four fingers to draw a big seven in front of her before swiping her hand across her forehead. Then she pointed at herself. *Promise me ... never forget me.*

He tapped his lips with an index finger and then used that hand, with the fingers spread apart, to cap over the thumb of another hand that was closed into a fist.

Chapter 6 Instinct

"The guys only bring very close friends or spouses to this party. And it's held at my friend's house, not some sleazy pubs. So it's just a relaxing get-together to chat and bond," explained Kiefer.

Even after his attempts to convince Elsie to join the gathering of his childhood friends, Elsie still rejected his invitation by shaking her head.

I rather bond with my data.

It was then she realized it had been quite a while she did not constantly think about work like she used to.

Shelving those thoughts aside, Elsie noticed the disappointment manifesting on Kiefer's face, thus feeling bad about it. However, the reclusive lady hated crowds, especially when they were mostly consisted of strangers. She could not compromise to mingle with his friends.

Kiefer attempted to wipe that look off his face by smiling brightly. Amazingly, his broad, charming smile had the ability to eclipse over any form of negativities. The momentarily downcast man appeared to have reverted to his blithesome self in an instant.

Assuming that he was not badly affected by her decision, Elsie breathed a soft sigh of relief. She proceeded to tap the phrase "Enjoy the party" on her board.

He bobbed his head though the ends of his lips formed a slight frown. "Sure ..." Then he mumbled, "Oh no, Jennifer will grab this chance to pounce on me. What a nuisance."

Catching what he had said, Elsie wrote, "Your childhood sweetheart?" on her whiteboard.

He immediately choked at seeing her question. Coughing to clear his throat and waving his hand, the panicking guy shook his head. He managed to squeeze out the words, “No way. I try to steer clear of her, but she keeps pestering me since high school.”

With a cheeky smile appearing on her face, she teased him by telling him through writing to give Jennifer a chance since she had tried so hard and for so long.

He furrowed his brows and wrinkled his nose in disgust as he confessed, "She's not my type. I knew that when I overheard her bragging that her Zumba dance practices were tougher than army's trainings.

The man then wasted no time to clarify, “And I’ve given my heart to ...” He started choking on air again.

Concerned, Elsie rushed up to pat his back, hoping that it might help him. *Is he going to say it? The care he has been showering on me goes beyond what a tour guide or a friend ... but ... maybe I shouldn’t think too much into it.*

“Do you want pizza?” he asked after the coughs were suppressed.

Huh? She could not believe he switched topic so abruptly.

“I can order for you, if you don’t want to go out for dinner.” He flashed a sheepish smile.

***

The moment Ioteidas arrived at the rendezvous point, Elsie, who was resting at the edge of the rock outcrop, got up and looked at him shyly. Not taking her eyes off him to ensure his full attention, she began to untie the chocolate-brown ribbons on the front of her wheat-white bohemian dress. Wanting to experience what it was like to swim in the sea without the drag of the clothes, just like he always did, she let her dress slid off onto the rocks.

Not wearing any undergarments, she stood before the man, baring her soul to him, ready for his taking. Despite being mentally prepared to shed it all off in front of him, she was hit by a wave of nervousness as he regarded her body intently, not saying a word, his jaws clenched. The chilling breeze that scudded across her skin remained her of the fact that she had nothing to hide behind. He could clearly read her thoughts from the state of arousal her body was in. As the cold cut into her bones, she shivered uncontrollably.

Noticing the trembling of the lithe feminine form before him, the man immediately offered, "Come, my goddess." He put out his hand. Flickers of unadulterated lust sparked in his eyes, imparting a soft, muted glow onto his preternatural blue irises.

The blushing, flattered woman lowered her head, rested her hand in his outstretched one before slowly sitting down to dip her feet into the water, unsure of what to expect.

He slid his arm under her bottom and embosomed her waist with another arm to lift her off the rocky surface.

Gasping in surprise, she threw her arms around his neck and propped her elbows on his shoulders to steady herself.

The man looked up to stare at Elsie in the eyes while loosening his hold slightly to let her slide down. The sheer sensation of her delicate body, especially at the sensitive areas, grazing against his hard, smooth, wet chest had her breathing out soft sighs of pleasure.

The moment her rosy lips were almost within his reach, he stretched up to voraciously shower incandescent kisses on her, alternating between sucking her lips and licking them. While she was indulging in the feel of his lips and tongue, he proceeded to adorn her cheek with light pecks. Then those progressed to soft nips on her ear. Every breath of his brushing against her ear was telling Elsie how much he wanted to make love with her, to consummate their love, and to get tangled in each other's world.

Then he twisted his body, and with a twirl, caused her to fall backward to float on the surface of the sea. With her head tilted back, fully exposing her neck, Ioteidas, who was on top of her with his tail in the water, was given free reins to titillate the sensitive skin of her neck ... her shoulders and her breasts.

The swishing of water reminded her of the precarious position she was in: she could easily fall headlong into the depths of the ocean since she was prone to sinking as her tensed up body was overcome by spasms of sybaritism due to the intense stimulus. Yet even the sea would think twice about pulling her down into its deadly embrace, for she was in the protective arms of her man, the ruler of the sea.

She felt his fingertips gliding across her skin as he moved his hands across her back and the soft contours of her chest. She was suspended in the ethereal eroticism where the reality of his touches and realm of transcendence merged together.

When he traced her belly button and then moved further down, she was thrusted into a whirlwind of sexual hedonism. She was ready to be one with him.

Unwilling to wait any longer, Elsie interlocked her fingers behind his neck and pulled herself up to kiss him on the lips furiously. He reciprocated with sheer ferocity, smashing all concerns to smithereens. However, in their passion, he was too absorbed in their exchanges of vows of love to prevent his sharp canine from slicing through the thin epidermis of her lower lip. The stinging pain caused her to withdraw away from him and press her palm over her lips to stem the bleeding.

Ioteidas' reaction was far more drastic: he suddenly recoiled from her as if a blinding fast, great force hit him in the stomach, pushing him back several metres away from her. Pressing his palms against his face, with his claws digging into his skin, he hunched his shoulders as the hunger and pain were taking over his being. Tortured, unearthly, petrifying growls resonated within his throat as his shoulders and chest raised and fell wildly and erratically. His claws slowly pierced through his skin and drew gruesome streaks of red down his handsome visage. As soon as those wounds appeared, his skin cells speedily regenerated and bridged over the torn epidermis and dermis.

Are you alright? The worried and shocked Elsie tried to swim to Ioteidas to check on him.

She was stopped dead in her tracks when he snapped up his head to glare at her.

Within his facial features distorted by excruciating pain, there were undiluted, unquenchable hunger and inconceivable desire to bath in full wrought-out carnage. Gone was that lover who protected. In its place was a monster that would slaughter all indiscriminately. The legends were not merely legends.

"Blood is what triggers the feasting."

Covering her mouth in horror, she sobbed. She was afraid, not for her life, but because she did not want him to lose himself and his sanity. She did not want to see him drowning in the perpetual abyss of pain and suffering. *You can fight it. Please....*

A sliver of her thoughts managed to tunnel into his head, causing the conflicted merman to bellow in agony. The water around them thrashed about agitatedly. The air molecules twitched in distress. Grabbing the sides of his head, Ioteidas writhed while burrowing into the water and disappearing from the sight of Elsie.

Chapter 7 Stranger

Watching the two-year-old kid in front hobbling down the stone path shaded by the canopy of rows of live oak trees, with her parents at each side, Elsie felt the envy welling up inside her. Besides becoming a marine geophysicist, she also aspired to be a loving mother, just like her mum. In Elsie's eyes, her mum was a woman who defied all odds and worked tirelessly to raise her only daughter to be an individual with the capability and tenacity to pursue her dreams, not hampered by what she had lost.

Naysayers had speculated that her mother was only trying to make up for that moment of distraction that led to the accident. But Elsie could feel the genuine love from her mum, thus throwing all the nasty assumptions out of the window.

"Those discouragements mean nothing if you have the faith in your ability to achieve your goals." Elsie never forgot her mum's advice, holding it close to her heart.

Can I be like mum to surmount all obstacles to pursue my beliefs? I did it for my aspirations, but in relationship where another person is involved.... Someone who reacts violently to the scent of blood.

When Kiefer took note of Elsie's focus on the child, he commented, "I like kids. They're innocent and have a zest for life. And they laugh easily."

She looked up at Kiefer and tilted her chin towards the kid before using her index fingers to draw vertical lines from under her eyes and down her cheeks to indicate crying.

Kiefer let out a burst of chuckle. "Oh yes. They cry easily too. But for a child borne out of the love between me"—his face and ears turned red—"and ... my wife, I can take it." He paused to give it a second thought and went on to add, "I'll try my best."

Elsie felt her soul being torn into two when she heard his heartfelt sentiments.

***

Instead of the usual place, Elsie chose to hang out at the sandy beach. Sitting on the berm of the shore, with her knees to her chest, the listless woman was unwilling and unable to whistle a single note. Emotionally confused, she was not sure if she was ready to face Ioteidas again. Staring at the sand drenched in seawater, she wished she could find the courage to face the truth.

I'd seen it all, been through it all. But this? Then again, who in the world needs to deal with a bloodthirsty boyfriend?

The rollers repeatedly rushed in and shored up the sand to cradle it in their gentle embrace. Enthralled by the beauty of the froth gambolling around her feet, Elsie did not notice a silent figure approaching from behind.

"Waiting for that condemned monster?" asked the stranger with a heavy accent and a scathing tone.

Despite the fact that no one would address her man as anything else, other than the terms: monster, demon, abomination, Elsie could not contain her indignation. With her delicate features contorted by demurral, she whipped around and looked up at the tall man standing behind her.

The sea breeze tugged at the man's wavy, shoulder-length platinum blond hair tied loosely at the back and swept his fringe across his face. Still, the piercing stare from the quixotic stranger's emerald-green eyes managed to thread through long strands of his fringe to cut through her rage and immediately turn the frown on her face into a petrified expression. She could detect a lust, a murderous one, emanating from those windows to the corrupted soul, and the smirk on his full rosy lips did little to convince her otherwise. His intricate beauty was like the fully bloomed rose, whose thorns were dipped in the toxic root extract of the deadly nightshade, created to entice the prey into the trap to kill her.

Elsie had an urge to run away, but the second she leaned forward, ready to get up, that seemingly malicious man had already settled down beside her. Feeling his warm breath stroking her cheek, she instinctively shrank away from him to keep an arm's length away from the malefic entity.

Observing his snobbish demeanour and his outfit of white irregular slim suit with standing collar and trousers of matching colour, completed with white leather shoes, she found it plain obvious that he was not from the village. *Who are you?*

With her eyes glued on him and her palms pushing against the bed of sand to stop herself from falling backward during the bid to maintain a "safe" distance between them, she clenched her hands and gathered the sand in her fists. The lady was prepared to throw the sand into his eyes if he dared to show a slight hint of aggression. *What else can I do? I can't even scream.* She began to tremble in frustration at her helplessness.

The man laughed at the sight before him and waved a hand dramatically. "Don't worry. I'll not finish you off"—he paused as an eyebrow of his arched up—"just yet. After all, you're a special one who had by pure chance evaded the hunters—most of them, to be precise. Perhaps aphonia, or should I say, the inability to produce voice is a blessing in disguise?"

Elsie's eyes widened further at his comments. *How did he know?*

He straightened his suit before continuing, "Maybe an introduction will ease this tension between us? I'm Jean from the House of Yves." Placing his right arm across the front of his waist, he made an exaggerated bow, like he was greeting the queen.

Then Jean looked up and stared at her in the eyes. "In fact, you should be more afraid of that monster. We, the rulers of the night, are created by The Scales for a noble purpose. As for him, he's just a bastard chimera of my kind and a low life demon that should have perished in the war that gave birth to this land we're stepping on."

Shaking her head furiously, Elsie sneered at his proclamation. *You're not comparable to him!*

"Hmm, still in denial." After wiggling his finger in a mocking manner and clicking his tongue, he advised, "You need to face the truth: he's truly one of those pathetic waterborne monstrosities crushed to defeat by one of the three heavenly warriors, the great Archmage—The Scales. The only reason that monster was spared when his brethren were extirpated was because he begged for mercy."

As if in the spirit of theatrics, he threw up his hands while making a loud sigh. "Alas, The Scales, a staunch believer in balance, not tilting towards either damnation or forgiveness, decided to bestow that loser with the gift, so that he could be the guard dog of the ocean to maintain the balance while redeeming himself through his guard duties."

Elsie put her clenched fist over her heart as she hunched, trying to disregard his venomous words ... and contemplating on hurling sand at his face. *So what? His association with The Scales doesn't make it worse than that well-spread legend. And that's the past, isn't it? What matters is now. I love him, I can put it aside.* Then her resolve was rattled violently when she remembered Ioteidas' malevolent glare after he tasted her blood.

With a confident glow on his face, Jean held out his hand to Elsie. "Come to me instead. I'll be far gentler, and it'll be less painful."

Staring at his outstretched fair hand and his fingers uncurling gracefully like the petals of a blooming flower, the lady was going to slap it away when Jean suddenly leaped away from her. A string of water droplets in the formation of a corkscrew tore through the space that Jean had vacated a split second ago. Those droplets spun through the air over a long stretch of beach before colliding into an Aleppo pine tree trunk, then drilling through the bark and cambium to destroy the thick layers of sapwood and heartwood and sever the trunk. Elsie froze in terror at witnessing the magnitude of destruction.

With inhuman speed and astonishing agility, Jean landed on an outcrop of rocks ten metres away from Elsie. His eyes were coruscating with excitement as he looked at the gigantic approaching wave. "I thought you'll only arrive long after she's gone."

Before Jean could further taunt his opponent, he was forced to jump away as a splash of water smacked into the rocks. The area within the vicinity was instantly flooded with seawater. And Elsie was swamped by the seawater, with only her head and shoulders above the water.

A tenebrous figure emerged from the turbulent waves, his teal blue eyes were glowing with unbridled rage. The veins across his arms, neck, chest and back were bulging madly. The gills on his torso flared with each forceful breath he exhaled. "I believe you're forbidden from hunting here. Unless time has been merciless on you, and you'd forgotten that this is the territory of Veit, not your lord's." Hidden within his even voice were the forcibly suppressed growls of an unhinged beast.

Jean smiled and brushed his fringe away from his face. "Ah, I never forget, even after centuries had passed. You can rest easy now. Is it the nature of a monster to kick up a fuss over a matter of nary a concern?"

"You're hardly a trustworthy individual knowing your boundaries. And it's well-known that nothing good comes out of your contact with humans." Ioteidas proceeded to swing his hand to draw an arc on the surface of the sea. The splashes of water, whose molecules were imbued with the unholy combination of demonic energy and the power given by an esteemed Archmage, spiralled towards Jean.

"How rude. As expected from a maladjusted being like you." Jean willed his transparent-looking French cavalry sword—one that was constituted of air molecules—to form in his hand and deftly sliced through those water bullets.

The next moment, more attacked him from the flank. He hopped sideway to avoid those deadly shots only to see Ioteidas suddenly bursting out of the water beside him. Those sharp claws of the dweller of the sea would have ripped out the front of Jean's throat if he did not cock his head backward in time. As the merman plunged back into the sea, Jean sprang away.

Elsie could only watch on in horror. She feared for Ioteidas' life, yet she also had no wish to witness him snuffing out a life just like that. *Got to get out of here. I can't bear to watch it. And I can't be in his way.* After getting up, with great effort, and gathering the skirt of her dress, she scampered away from the site of battle.

Darting down the length of the beach and parrying all attacks that came his way, Jean complained, "You almost ruined my suit. Had you even considered on whether you had the means to compensate for it when you tried that move?"

Streaking across the water along the coast in pursuit of Jean, Ioteidas replied in an acrimonious manner, "I don't need to pay if you're dead."

"Oh, and you don't need to pay if you become a fish with its belly up," chirped Jean. "But before that ..."—he slid to the lady hiding behind a huge boulder and put his arm around her—"ah, Mademoiselle, had you made your choice? Take note that it'll affect your lifespan."

Ioteidas skidded to a violent stop as he looked on in seething anger and utter fear at the terrified Elsie palpitating and staring at him with pleading eyes. He intently tracked Jean's movements, ready to pull out all stops to protect his woman.

Jean, whose eyes were sparkling with glints of sadistic mischief and were firmly on his enemy, whispered into Elsie's ear, loud enough for Ioteidas to catch every word, "The whiffs of arousal surrounding your body are too obvious to be ignored. When it comes to fulfilling your wish, yes, hidden beneath the shark skin, he's a man in every sense, having the ability to deflower you."

"Leave her alone. This is between us!" commanded Ioteidas as he inched closer to the two.

Ignoring the merman and the overpowering malice that hung around him, Jean continued in a leisurely tone, "But the child conceived will be like him, possessing a hunger for blood. Being a messy eater, it'll chew on your flesh in a frenzy to get what it needs. When you, the vessel, die, so will the one in your womb."

Looking at Ioteidas, Elsie shook her head in disbelief and denial. *This is not true, right?*

However, his solemn silence shattered her hopes.

Smiling in fiendish delight, Jean proposed, "Whereas with me, it'll be painless. If you pleasure me well enough, I might consider taking you in as my immortal consort instead."

Elsie tore her eyes off the man in the water and through her tear-filled eyes, glowered at Jean. With despondency superseding her fear, she pushed him away. *Get away from me. I'd seen it all, been through it all. Your tricks will not work on me. All you creatures be gone!*

Jean shrugged in mocked resignation. "Too bad—"

He was cut off when a vertical wave of water was launched towards him in the blink of an eye, threatening to carve him into halves. Just ducking the assault in the nick of time, he could hardly take a breather before another vicious wave closed in for the kill.

The merman kept on unleashing wave after wave of attacks, forcing the blond to retreat and back off from the defenceless human.

Just when it seemed like Ioteidas was not going to stop until Jean was sliced into pieces, a brunette in dark green intricate silk gown and black lace gloves rushed in from nowhere to block the fatal projectiles with a transparent umbrella.

Widening his eyes in surprise, Ioteidas halted his attacks and warily eyed the new intruder.

Dusting his suit, Jean exclaimed, "Oh, Sophia, the beautiful pearl of the House, welcome to the beach party."

Regarding her brethren with disapproval and letting her umbrella dissipated into ordinary air molecules, Sophia went on to throw a glance of disgust at Ioteidas. Though her expressions softened for a split second when her meticulously outlined eyes lingered on the contours of Ioteidas' muscular chest.

Then taking a deep breath, she flicked her perfectly coiffed curly hair away from her shoulder, rested her hands on the hips with utter feminine grace and announced, "I'll inform Lord Yves of what had transpired here. You'll not encounter Jean around here for a long time to come."

"Ah, barred from another place," grumbled Jean, who was oddly smiling.

Not bothering to wait for any sign of acknowledgement, Sophia warned Elsie sinisterly to keep her mouth shut on the encounters with Jean and her before whirling around to stomp off to the village. "Trust you to muddle around with a human and a deviate," she chided through clenched teeth, not slowing down once to look back at anyone.

Jean followed closely behind and waved a hand while retorting, "The boredom of staying in that antiquity needs to be warded off through the introduction of some excitement. Or else the ghosts of the past will catch up to me."

Sophia narrowed her eyes and snapped, "Excitement? I can give you that by cutting off your head when you've gotten weak from giving the gift to your new pet."

"That will be so not honourable," he reminded.

She almost rolled her eyes. "Etiquette is my sole concern. I know no honour. You can have it when duelling with Slade."

Jean immediately snorted in apprehension. "That brute ..."

As the two unworldly ones disappeared into the darkness, Elsie felt the water level rising up to her chest while Ioteidas was swimming to her. Instinctively putting up her hands in front of her face, the forlorn and traumatized woman recoiled from him when he sought to embrace her in order to comfort her.

Sobbing uncontrollably, Elsie wanted to lunge into his arms. However, she was also afraid. *I can't take it anymore.*

With his eyes darkening in disappointment, Ioteidas realized that the only comfort he could bring to his love was to leave her. Spinning around, he dived into the sea and vanished in the cold, black water.

Chapter 8 Demon

After an early dinner in a fancy Italian restaurant within a small five-storey hotel—the only hotel in the village, Kiefer and Elsie promenaded along the well-trodden dirt path, through an open field to get to her resort. Though Elsie was initially feeling downcast and conflicted, Kiefer managed to brighten up her mood with stories on the crazy things he had done while on duty. Using cell phone to get fresh water through distillation of seawater, trying to communicate with the whales by mimicking their vocalizations, pretending the dog on board the ship to be a tiger stranded with him on an imaginary tiny boat, and playing out the famous lovers' scene at the head of the ship—the retelling of those light-hearted moments put a smile on Elsie's face.

Noticing that the lady was warming up to him, Kiefer suddenly halted in the middle of the path. Elsie regarded him with a bemused expression.

Gazing into her eyes, he pointed at her and proceeded to tap his chest once. Then he put his fists together, palm to palm, and moved his hands horizontally to draw a circle in the air.

With her mouth dropping slightly open in astonishment, the touched and stunned Elsie tried to reconcile with the fact that Kiefer had went all out to learn sign language to confess his desire to be together with her.

Seeing no sign of apprehension on Elsie's face, the guy summoned his courage and grabbed the opportunity to reach over and plant a light kiss on her parted lips.

It was a sweet and blissful kiss that filled Elsie with warm, fuzzy feelings and a sense of security. Confused and undecided, she had no clue on how to react.

Gently clasping her hands, he said, "Give me time to learn sign language. I'll master it, so there's no more barrier between us. I'm going to set sail three days later, and I need to catch the bus tomorrow to get to the base. So ... will you wait for me?" Gleams of hope and sincerity were shining in his eyes.

Elsie wished she could just say "yes". For she could imagine the cosy love nest they would forge together. Holding hands while strolling along the beach, laughing over his jokes, encouraging each other through difficulties of life, nurturing their children and spending their twilight years together, those were right within the grasp of her hands at that precise moment.

However, she could not shove aside her pining for the man languishing in the cold, lonely darkness of the ocean. Her dreams were haunted by images of him, nevertheless giving her a small moment of happiness while she was detached from reality. But it was cruelly snatched away when she woke up. Her heart ached terribly at the memories of him—refreshed every night for the past few days. However, she was terrified of laying her eyes on the atrocities he would commit. She wanted to live in denial that she had merely fallen in love with a misunderstood man, not a monster capable of taking away lives at a flick of his finger.

She craved for a normal life. *Is it fair for Kiefer? He can be with a girl who's hundred percent devoted to him.*

Swallowing hard and avoiding eye contact with Kiefer, Elsie went on to pen down her decision on the whiteboard she had been holding onto.

A slight gloom cloaked his face when he saw her answer. Then blinking his eyes, he ruffled his hair while chuckling awkwardly. "Sure, no problem"—he shrugged—"it's good to think it through before deciding. I'll delay the schedule of boarding the bus by a day.... I want to hear it from you personally."

With her eyes tearing up, she smiled in appreciation of his willingness to wait for her.

***

A grey, monstrous figure erupted from the sea in front of the chained woman. She went weak with revulsion and fear, unable to utter a single word upon sighting the hideous creature looming before her.

A chimera with only its torso and skull resembling those of a human, its lower body was that of a shark, and its head was an abomination that could only exist in the most warped nightmares. Its whole body was covered in abnormally abrasive shark skin that could easily scrape the skin off a human's body. Those bready, turquoise demonic eyes, swollen with menace and insanity, were glowing and casting a ghostly greenish blue tint on its grotesque facial features: huge pointed ears with sharp tips that were equipped to slice off fingers, wide mouth with the ends almost touching the ears, and numerous rows of razor-sharp, serrated teeth lined the fresh red gums. The three rows of spikes that ran from its forehead and down the spine were long and sharp enough to impale a man. That monstrosity was the notorious creature that had fed on countless of maidens before her—*Ioteidas.*

When she squeezed her eyes shut, too scared to witness her own impending doom, a harpoon sailed through the air, aiming for the monster's head. The creature glided away with ease to avoid the weapon.

"Stay away from my woman!" yelled a black-haired man as he jumped down the rocky slope, with a dagger in his hand.

Her eyes widened in disbelief at the man's arrival. She could not believe that he came to save her when he had cut her off from his life ever since she had been chosen to be the sacrifice. He did not protest against the decision, accepting it in an unnaturally calm manner—not that his objection would change the elders' minds. Neither did he strive to make the best out of her last days. He did not even show up during the procession to send her off. She thought he had abandoned her to her predicament.

"No, Alastair!" she implored, not wanting him to die in futile. *Why didn't the elders stop him?*

With his back to the lady, the man paid no heed to her warning and had his entire focus on the demon.

Watching Alastair agilely hopping around and swiping at his enemy, without much success, she found the answer to her question when she saw the blood smeared on the dagger's blade and the harpoon. And her feet were soaked in the blood that flowed down from the top of the slope.

With each second passed, more gnashing wounds appeared on Alastair's body. The lightning-fast creature darted around in the water, apparently holding back its killing move, like it was taunting the human that his life was at its mercy. However, the stinging, intense pain only served to remind Alastair not to let his woman suffered the same fate, driving him closer to madness and amplifying his obsession to slay the monster. Leaping to the stuck harpoon, whose tip was wedged between the rocks, he proceeded to exert all of his strength to pull it out.

Wielding two weapons, he viciously and relentlessly attacked the creature, not caring if his blood was pouring out of his lacerations.

His tenacity finally paid off when he managed to jam the harpoon into the demon's shoulder. When the blade was yanked out of the flesh, the cacodemon's scarlet red blood was sprayed all over the man. Feeling revitalized after his successful attack, Alastair charged at his foe to land more hits with his dagger. As the fiend was shrieking in pain, the human jumped towards it to plunge the harpoon deep into its heart.

The immobilized woman could not help noticing that the monster was laughing while drawing its last breaths. "I'm free," it gurgled.

Though when the lifeless corpse of the creature collapsed, Alastair was not taking pride in his near impossible feat. Instead, he was clutching his head in excruciating pain and trembling violently. His grunts of pain slowly transformed into deep, inhuman growls.

"Alastair, are you okay?" shouted the concerned woman.

He responded by whipping around to glare at her.

That chiselled face ... the Alastair of the past was the Ioteidas of the present.

She realized with uneasiness that his brown irises were changing to the same colour as the eyes of the fiend slain, his canines had become longer and sharper, his lips and nails were turning black, and his hair was rapidly growing longer.

Drawing ragged breaths and eyeing the woman, Alastair could no longer control his bloodlust. His sanity was grinded into fragments as a thousand years of avalanche of knowledge and memories inundated his mind. The creature's blood cells multiplied and devoured the human's blood cells running in the man to colonize the veins and arteries. His transmuted, unholy cells were calling for fresh human blood to feed on so as to complete the metamorphosis.

Pouncing onto her, he sank his teeth into her jugulars.

He could not register the pleas and dying throes of his love. All he could discern was his need to satisfy his hunger.

Alastair....

The extreme pain and absolute horror ripped Elsie out from her dreams. Jolting up from the bed, she clenched her teeth at the fresh pain assaulting her neck.

Then she saw the wraith-like face of a beautiful woman floating before her, only few centimetres from face contact. Shocked by the sudden appearance of the apparition, she felt a shortness of breath, and her limbs refused to move one bit. The ghost smiled and whispered into Elsie's ear before evanescing.

Where had I heard that voice before?

Flashed across her head was the memory of a soft voice, heard within the rustling of the wind, warning her to steer clear of the water and the sandy areas on the first night she started whistling her tunes to the sea. Assuming that it was just a figment of her imagination, Elsie did not give much thought to it.

And it was the voice of the poor soul butchered by her lover in Elsie's nightmares.

Throwing aside the blanket, Elsie wasted no time to dash out of her room and head out to the coast. The bare-footed woman in pyjamas kept on running towards the shoreline in the dead of the night, not stopping once to take a break. When she reached her destination, drenched in cold sweat, she looked at the dark untraversable sea and wished frantically that she had a voice to call out for Ioteidas.

No, I can't give up. I must see him!

She waded into the water and shivered as coldness ate into her flesh, and the ghosts within the sea fled at the sight of her.

I can't stop until he's here.

Forcing her breath through her blue lips to emit eldritch high-pitched sounds in the midst of chattering teeth, she forced her legs to march forward even when her body longed for a rest.

I need to know.

Her calls were finally answered when her head was going underwater. The sea receded promptly to her waist, and a turbulence within the ocean barrelled towards Elsie. Ioteidas broke out of the surface of the water and without a word and hesitation, wrapped his arms around the quivering lady to impart his warmth to her.

"I thought you'll never come," he spoke in a hushed voice.

Tears streamed down her cheeks as she realized the prodigious extent of her craving for his touches.

When she started to choke on her tears, Ioteidas gently pulled away and looked at her in the eyes. The moment he saw her face, the concern in his eyes was tempered with consternation.

Pressing her lips tightly together, the lady used hand signs to reveal the truth that could spell the death of hope. *You're the man who slew the sea monster to save your love in that legend about the Hero of Bantora, isn't it? You were once human.*

Pressing his palm against the side of his forehead, he shook his head while trying to prise out the lost memories buried deep within his mind. "I've no impression ..."

After the battle, you transformed into what you are now and drank her blood. Elsie hammered the forgotten facts into his head.

He froze at the disclosure and sudden sharp pain drilling into his brain. "Amara ..." he mumbled.

Elsie furiously nodded in confirmation, for the ghost had mentioned the exact same name to her. Then she pointed her right finger at the vacant space on her right before brushing her fingertips along the length of her palm twice. The lady finished what she was tasked to say by pointing at Ioteidas.

He smiled bitterly. "She'd forgiven me? What difference does it make? I feel nothing about it. I can't remember." Gritting his teeth and biting his tongue in the process, he lamented, "Only the name and that guilt remain."

She forced out a smile and cradled his cheeks. *It's okay. Let's put this behind and start anew. All these are too much for a man to take, I want to share the burdens with you. I'm not going to get deterred by the setbacks anymore. Amara ... she ... had shown me—*

"But I'm not a human," he spat. "The past had taught us that it's impossible. No matter how much you're willing to compromise. Your tears betray your feelings: the doubts in your heart."

She quickly employed sign language to tell him, "Give me time. I'll try to understand."

"How do you pin hopes on a man who had preyed on his lover ... and felt no remorse over it?" he interrogated with seething anger.

She shook her head. *You did feel remorse. You chose to abstain from blood and go into deep sleep ... isn't it due to the trauma of ...*

His eyes were saturated with sadness and resolve as he confessed, "I'm sorry to let my selfishness took precedence over everything else and dragged you into this. I should have kept you away. I can't repeat the same mistake again. I'll not be able to live with it if I end up hurting you."

The instance he finished his say with a kiss on her cheek, a huge wave crashed in to push Elsie to the berm of the beach. She wanted to go after him, but he just seemed to get further away from her.

Chapter 9 Blood

Staring out listlessly at the currents of the ocean rocking the small, white, blue-striped catamaran passenger ferry she was on, Elsie did her utmost to appreciate the beauty of the dark blue sea, displayed in full glory under the bright morning sun. Though it only reminded her of what lay beneath the surface. Even the friendly and cheerful tourists could not distract her for long from sinking into the sea of memories. It did not help that her stomach was feeling queasy.

Above the whirring of the engine, Elsie could hear a young couple humming softly to themselves and indulging in each other's company, several tourists gasping in wonderment at the tranquil and beautiful scenery around them, cameras clicking, and excited youngsters burbling.

Inhaling the fresh briny air that the gentle sea breeze brought forth into the open-air cabin of the boat, she tried to convince herself to just enjoy the moment of repose. *Come on, Elsie. Look at these fun-loving, carefree folks. Try to get the maximum out of this trip. Nothing can get you down, right?*

Then the loud groaning of the motors of an approaching patrol ship crushed through the jovial vibe around the tour boat. The ship's gigantic PA system repeatedly blared warnings about the ferry trespassing Mercales' territorial waters.

Questions flew between the bewildered tourists as they attempted to grasp the concept that they were not sailing on Accastle's waters, despite being not far off from the Southwest coast of Accastle. Assaulted by a sense of foreshadowing, the captain of the catamaran sent a distress signal to the control station in Bantora Village, notwithstanding the fact that hardly anyone was stationed there.

Badly affected by the tense atmosphere, the continuous exchange of words around her ears and the incessantly loud noises from the patrol ship, Elsie was starting to feel nauseous. She squatted down on the wooden floor and tucked her face between her knees.

The second Elsie huddled up against the black plastic legs of her seat, countless of bullets rained onto the small tour boat and yielded splatters of blood and bits of flesh when perforating the bodies of the tourists and boat captain. A minute seemed like an eternity as Elsie watched in wide-eyed horror the merciless obliteration of almost everyone on board. Even when most were riddled with bullet wounds, and there was no obvious sign of life among them, the barrage of bullets did not stop until the patrol guards had gotten tired of the "game" and were ready to check their spoils. Elsie was only spared because of the shields provided by the seats and a lifeless body of her neighbour—to think he had just asked how she was ten minutes ago.

Knowing that those guards would get on board the ferry soon, she quickly lay down, pulled the corpse over her face while mentally apologizing to him and then closed her eyes, pretending to be dead.

"Search through all areas thoroughly. We must find the corpse of the wanted spy and gather all the intelligence and evidence he has on him," barked one of the senior officers when he embarked onto the tour boat.

Elsie had a very bad feeling about staying hidden until the coast was clear, if the guards did not just stop at a quick scan of the boat. True enough, her facade was exposed when a patrol guard kicked the dead body off her and studied her face.

"Hey, this one seems alive." He was proven right with a tight slap across her cheek, causing her to flinch.

After the announcement, the other guards gathered around Elsie to ogle at her with leering eyes and began to debate on whether to take her back or finish her off after they were done with her.

Elsie clenched her fists while shaking in anger.

One noticed her reactions and mocked, "Scared? Then beg us." When she ignored him, he roughly pulled her hair and shouted, "Come on, say something. Are you mute?"

Though revolted by the crude laughter surrounding her, she could only give him the death stare. Feeling insulted, he gave her a swift kick in the stomach and took delight in watching her squirmed in agony and coughed muffled croaks of pain. Several others joined in the fray.

"Playing possum, huh? Stupid wretch!"

A young guard finally voiced his concern, "Aren't you guys going overboard? We're coast guards, not ruffians, right?"

An older man spat on the floor and replied with arrogance, "Don't worry. The higher-ups gave us the go-ahead to do anything we want."

Glaring at her assailants, Elsie wrenched a broken piece of hard plastic off a nearby tattered chair to stab the foot of the nearest guard with the sharp, ragged end of her weapon.

"Bitch!" cursed a comrade of the injured guy as he swung his fist at her jaws.

An inhuman, stentorian, earth-shattering roar rattled through the air and agitated the water. The guards glanced around nervously, wondering if it was the fabled monster that haunted the east of Atlantic Ocean.

"We'll make a beehive out of him if he appears," joked a man amid the unnerving situation.

As if in defiance to his boastful comment, a succession of violent waves were unleashed to ram the boat, sending the coast guards flailing wildly, with some falling over the edge of the ferry and into the raging sea below. As the young coast guard was treading water to stay afloat, he saw a mass of water churning madly and speeding towards him. Before he could raise his arm to swim away, that body of thrashing water swarmed around him. Sharp pain followed. Blood spread rapidly around him, and he realized that he was sinking, for he had no legs to paddle. While drowning in the ocean, he saw the upper lobe of a tail fin slicing through his officer cleanly at the chest. Two more had their upper bodies separated from the lower ones in a flash. He never knew coast guards could meet such grisly ends. *Damn, this is my first day at work....*

A guard was reaching for the side of the boat, with some of his colleagues on board giving him a hand. Out of the blue, Ioteidas surfaced behind that coast guard and thrusted his claws into the neck and shoulder of the doomed human. The merman went on to forcefully rip off part of the neck from the base before sinking his teeth into the torn flesh and jugular vein to guzzle on the long-craved-for blood.

The ones on the boat, not used to dealing with an enemy who was more offensive and powerful than them, recoiled at grotesque scene before them and then started fumbling with their rifles to take aim at the brute. Though the demon had dragged the dying man into the depths of the ocean, disappearing from their sight when they were ready to fire. After several seconds, Ioteidas leaped out of water and twisted his body to swing his tail at five guards looking over the hull. One slice was all that was needed to lop off their torsos. When the freshly slain ones were collapsing into a heap, the deranged monster snatched one of them off the boat to feast on it.

Elsie stared at her man in morbid fascination as she observed his veins bulging and pulsating madly, which was eerily similar to the phenomena in her dream where he was transforming into the very creature he had slaughtered. And irrepressible madness was cavorting in his eyes. Splashes of red were liberally poured over the nightmarish canvas before her, and the grim cacophony of screams of death bombarded her ears. Firearms had no effect on Ioteidas, for he easily decimated the bullets, the rifles and their wielders to shreds by shooting shards of water at them. Gathering her courage, she weakly stood up, wanting to go up to him and stop him. However, with a wave of his hand, a rush of water shoved her boat backward, impeding the woman from getting close.

No, stop it. Get a grip.

If her silent pleas could reach him through the wind, he would blatantly disregard them anyway, for his entire psyche was consumed by hunger and the appetite for bloodbath.

Through the dying throes, the blasts, the roars of the waves and the sharp, grating noises of the coast guard vessel being segmented by Ioteidas' attacks, Elsie could hear the furious grinding of an engine. Whirling around, she saw Kiefer rocketing towards her in a speedboat. And in his hand was a harpoon. Before she could signal to Kiefer to back off, he jumped off his boat seconds before a swipe of water cleaved through the centre of the boat.

When Kiefer vanished under the water, Elsie saw the fin of a shark looming around there. Then a surge of blood rose up from beneath the surface.

Clutching her hair in panic, she frantically scanned the sea for any signs of life. *Please let both of them be okay.*

All of a sudden, a pair of hands grabbed onto the edge of the hull of the catamaran. Startled, Elsie stumbled backward to see Kiefer, who looked to be unharmed, climbing up onto the boat.

Hurrying to the shocked lady, Kiefer, whose face was lined with worry, blurted, "Thank God you're alright. I was going crazy when received the distress call. The monster had gotten away. Come on, let's get you to safety before it attacks again." He grabbed Elsie's hand, guiding her to the lifeboat and hoping to lead her to a safe enclave.

Feeling comforted at the touch of Kiefer's warm hand, she smiled at him. The next moment, the corner of her eye caught the movement of a bullet careering towards them.

The tiny piece of metal pierced into Kiefer's temple at the side and spiralled through his head.

Those deep brown eyes that were always filled with hope, zest ... and adoration when set upon Elsie—they turned lifeless in an instant. Only void existed within them.

Devastated, Elsie caught hold of the falling Kiefer and cried at the top of her *voice*, hoping to summon him back to the mortal realm. Despite straining her vocal cords until they almost burst, only hoarse choking sounds came out of her. As the weight of Kiefer's body was taking a toll on Elsie, her legs finally buckled under the stress. Even after falling down, she refused to let go. Quickly propping an elbow against the floor to get up to sitting position, she held on tightly to Kiefer, mourning for him and swearing to protect his shell until her last breath. Looking at the sea in daze and rocking back and forth, she whistled a tune to send him off to another world.

Nothing else mattered at that moment. Facing away from the patrol ship and locking herself in a trance to block out the cruel reality and the ongoing horrors, she was impervious to everything, from the bullets zipping around, to the pitiful, incessant implorations of the survivors, including two officials hiding in the ship. Neither did she care about how they were violently butchered by the demon as he slashed their mouths to shut them up.

When serenity settled onto the sea once more, with only Elsie's song twirling with the shushing of the sea currents, Ioteidas called out for his love and cut through her self-imposed barricade. She finally saw why Ioteidas had warned her to stay away when they had first met. He was truly a monster capable of committing heinous acts beyond her imagination. Yet she could not toss away her love for him even at that revelation. And she truly and thoroughly understood his feelings of carrying those burdens and guilt on his shoulders, for she was in the same shoes right then.

Lying Kiefer carefully down on the floor, she planted a kiss on his cold forehead. *Wait for me.*

Then turning around with trepidation, she crawled on trembling limbs to Ioteidas, who was hovering by the side of the boat, his chest above the water. The insanity in his eyes was slowly displaced by regret, guilt and intense pain.

The instant Elsie reached the edge of the boat, she leaned over it without hesitation to stretch out her hands towards Ioteidas. In response, he gripped the top of the hull with a hand and lifted himself up to be at eye level with his woman.

Using another hand to grab her by the back of her neck, he pulled her into his embrace and locked his lips over hers. That contact of lips felt exactly like the first one they had, and just like that time, while being overwhelmed by ambivalence and fear, she relished the kiss.

Seconds ticked by, and he suddenly let go of her and plunged back into the reddish water. With a sorrowful smile on his face, he said, "I wish I could have done this earlier. But I didn't have that power."

Gazing at Elsie with fervent longing, he called forth the combers to send the ferry drifting in the direction of the shoreline. She tried to get a hold on him, but the distance between them widened by metres with each passing second. And with a spin, he dived into the ocean—his haven of solitude and isolation.

Heartbroken, Elsie cried out loud for him. Crisp, fragile voice punctured the heavy atmosphere. It was the first time her crying was audible, but there was no one around to respond to it.

Chapter 10 Song

A soft, beautiful glow was smudged into the surrounding serene darkness by the warm, dandelion-yellow light that washed through the double hung colonial style windows of the rustic dune shack of the Knights. The humble house was bursting with ebullient energy and mirthful laughter as the family gathered around the long wooden dining table for Christmas Eve dinner, talking, joking and chatting loudly. It had been quite a while since the elderly Knight, Chris, saw his sons, thus he was elated to have them with him, even if it was for a week only.

One chair at the corner remained empty throughout the meal because it was meant for Kiefer, and his position and importance in the family was irreplaceable. Sometimes, short moments of sorrow mantled the place when Kiefer was mentioned. All of them missed the carefree, courageous guy terribly. However, most of the time, they reminisced fondly and happily about the great time they had with him, his episodes of bravery and his misadventures. They all unanimously agreed that he represented hope and joy, no less.

Seated beside that empty chair was Elsie, who was there because Chris had regarded her as part of the family. She was after all the very person who stuck around with him for the last five years since that tragedy, making it a point to have dinner with him every single day without fail. That was the only way Elsie felt she could redeem herself. Nevertheless, the sense of redemption could not cast off the guilt she had to carry for eternity. The nature of her job and the availability of advanced communication tools made it possible for her to be based in Bantora while collecting data from all over the world and getting the analysis done.

Though she had a voice already, due to habit, she did not contribute much to the conversations. Listening intently to others, smiling or laughing in response, she was glad to be in the company of such jovial folks. When all had finished their dinner, she, as usual, offered to clean up the table and wash the dishes. But the younger Knights and their wives insisted on helping out. After all chores were done, she bade farewell, ready to let the Knights spent some quality family time together. The friendly peeps said reluctant goodbyes to her, but they understood that it was too dangerous to hang out late at night in the vicinity.

After promising to visit them the next day, she trotted down the limestone brick pavement, heading to her home. But she only went back to have a quick bath, as per her inveterate routine. When she had refreshed herself after a day of working in front of the computer and then going down to accompany Chris, she made her way to the beach, like she did every night. Along the way, she received a call on her handphone from a suitor, and as typical of her, she rejected his invitation without hesitation. In fact, she had closed her doors to all her suitors, regardless of everything.

When she reached her destination, she cautiously tiptoed down a slope made up of rocks to get to the protruding rocky platform flanked by the Atlantic Ocean.

Then ensconcing herself on the rock outcrop and taking in a deep inhale of the briny air, she closed her eyes to appreciate her surroundings through other senses. As the emotions welled up inside her, she began to release them through whistling.

The lady was not expecting anyone. Her sole motivation to sing was to soothe the pain of the man dwelling in the depths of the ocean. She believed that he was out there somewhere, fulfilling his calling to protect the ocean. Her belief was borne five years ago when she read the report on Mercales' *man-made island* being filleted within minutes. And that very belief was affirmed with news on the exceedingly high death tolls in the contested waters—to the point where no one survived to be eyewitness to determine the identity of the perpetrator. There were unexplainable destruction of military ships, dredges, frigates, submarines and massive fishing fleets sailing around there. Yet the environmentalists, tourists, adventurers, occasional patrol vessels of Accastle and even the fishermen on small boats venturing into those dangerous zones did not encounter any out of ordinary occurrences.

She wondered about how much he had changed in appearance, along with the powers he had gained. However, she had no chance of finding out, for he had never appeared before her again. Still, she wanted to be there for him always.

Indulging in the seamless melody of her tunes entwining gracefully with the susurration of the sea, she did not notice the sudden rise in tide.

Her eyes flew open when the loud splashing of water pounded her eardrums. She immediately quivered with shock and excitement and was choked by a rush of vehemence hitting her right in the heart as she saw a figure surfacing from the sea near the rock outcrop she was sitting on.

Hovering in the water before her was the man she had been pining for. His appearance had, strangely, not changed one bit since she had last seen him. Hundreds of years of hibernating and resisting his hunger had imprinted their mark on his very core.

For a moment, she could not move. Tears gushed out of her eyes as she cupped her mouth with both hands. She yearned so much for him to rush over and seize her into his arms.

However, only bewilderment and annoyance existed in his narrowed eyes. "Who are you? What's your purpose in calling for me?" he bellowed.

You still remember.... With a look of resolve on her face, Elsie quickly stood up and jumped into the sea while reaching out for him. She managed to get a hold on his shoulder and pulled herself up before fully submerging in the water.

He regarded her with interest. "Such temerity ..."

She pressed her lips firmly over his, her free arm snaked around his neck to pull the man closer, not letting him go.

Promise me ... never forget me.

As if by instinct, he enfolded her tightly in his arms.

The End

Afterword

Thank you very much for reading my book. I hope you had enjoyed reading it.

This book was actually inspired by a drawn portrait of a beautiful man bursting out of the water. The moment I set my eyes on it, my mind exploded with a slew of ideas, stemming from various sources: horror movies, video games, National Geographic and news on current affairs. With the ambition to portray a merman as a beautiful, graceful, ethereal yet fearsome creature, I combined these ideas and the world I had created in my previous novels to write this story.

As to how Elsie and Ioteidas overcome the obstacles after this, that is for them to work it out. All I can say is that their ordeals make them stronger. In the second novella of *The Forbidden* series, *Beast within The Man*, we will embark on a new journey to explore the relationship between a woman and ... a werewolf. So stay tuned.

If you are wondering what Jean and Sophia are, well, they do have the same bloodlust that infects Ioteidas. Sophia even makes a short, brief appearance in my novel, *Blood or Flesh*.

So till next time.

Bises.

About the Author

Shaine Lake may seem like the unlikely candidate to write romance novels, given her background of reading Dungeons and Dragons books, HP Lovecraft's novels, Junji Ito's works, heart-warming stories about animals and news regarding politics, culture and science.

She ventured into novel writing, namely in the genres of Romance and Action, not only seeking to inject refreshing concepts and crazy ideas into the said genres, and also to fulfil her desire:

To incite intense emotions in readers. To make them swoon, laugh, cringe, sob and ponder.

Her route to achieve these is through her tales that combine fantasy, paranormal romance, sensuality and furious action.

www.ingramcontent.com/pod-product-compliance
Lightning Source LLC
LaVergne TN
LVHW091039150826
845672LV00006BA/1892